"Am I rushing you, Sugar?" Powers murmured in her ear

Blair sank back woozily on the sofa. "It may be that we both are rushin' things. We barely know each other, after all." Thank heaven her accent was still intact. Little else was. She tugged her skirt down. She couldn't seem to remember why wanting him was a bad idea. . . .

He leaned closer. "The world falls away for both of us when we're together, Sugar. I feel it. I know you feel it too."

Blair's lips still stung from their kiss. She brushed a strand of hair away. Dear Lord, what if Powers had furrowed his fingers through her false hair?

She couldn't run the risk of discovery. "Maybe we should cool it, Powers."

"I'll try," he said agreeably, placing one hand on her knee. He smiled rakishly. His wicked fingers edged slowly upward. "How am I doing, Sugar?"

Blair's heart pounded. She felt hot all over. "Not cool enough," she said breathlessly.

While in college, **Roseanne Williams** worked the St. Francis Hotel's front desk in San Francisco. Fondly recalling her wacky experiences, she decided to write a romance about the intricacies of the hotel business. *Under the Covers* is a rollicking tale in which Roseanne's heroine is subjected to Murphy's Law: Whatever can go wrong, does! Watch for Roseanne's next book, *The Bad Boy*, in our Rebels & Rogues miniseries, Temptation's 1992 salute to heroes.

Books by Roseanne Williams

HARLEQUIN TEMPTATION
237—HOW SWEET IT IS!
306—THE MAGIC TOUCH
350—LOVE CONQUERS ALL

Don't miss any of our special offers. Write to us at the following address for information on our newest releases.

Harlequin Reader Service
P.O. Box 1397, Buffalo, NY 14240
Canadian address: P.O. Box 603,
Fort Erie, Ont. L2A 5X3

Under the Covers
ROSEANNE WILLIAMS

Harlequin Books

TORONTO • NEW YORK • LONDON
AMSTERDAM • PARIS • SYDNEY • HAMBURG
STOCKHOLM • ATHENS • TOKYO • MILAN
MADRID • WARSAW • BUDAPEST • AUCKLAND

Published February 1992

ISBN 0-373-25484-9

UNDER THE COVERS

1

"NO ONE WOULD EVER guess you're you now." Blair Sansome was talking to herself in front of her full-length bedroom mirror. "Including Powers Knight."

She adjusted the brown wig that concealed her short, sleek black hair. Brown contact lenses masked her wideset, sea-green eyes.

"Even face-to-face or nose-to-nose, no one would guess." She slipped on non-prescription glasses with thick tortoise-shell frames. "Not that you'll be rubbing noses with Powers ever again."

She stepped back and assessed the disguise she had pulled together on short notice. With her hair now brown and shoulder-length with bangs instead of short and black, her nails trimmed instead of long, her polish clear instead of red, her brown wool suit stodgy instead of stylish, her brown heels stacked instead of spiked, the reflection in the mirror bore little resemblance to her usual self.

Temporarily wrinkling her skin would have been too difficult, so Blair looked her age—not the vibrant, striking twenty-seven she was, but an inconspicuous twenty-seven in a plain brown wrapper.

Turning in a slow circle, Blair checked herself out from every angle. Powers had worshipped her legs that night five years ago, but very little of them showed below the mid-calf hem of her skirt.

Facing the mirror, she smiled. Perfect. The telltale space between her two front teeth was hidden by a temporary concealer.

Last, Blair cleared her throat and resurrected the southern accent of her native New Orleans. Living in Seattle since her childhood had de-southernized her speech. "Thaink yew sew muhtch," she drawled. "Ah dew appreciate it."

More certain than ever that no one she knew would recognize her, she left her bedroom to test her accent on Angel Clare. For him, she'd lay it on honey-thick.

"Angellll," she drawled as she walked into the kitchen. "Good Monday mornin', darlin' bird." She plucked the cover from his white wicker cage.

"Aaaaccckkk!" the little cockatiel screeched in alarm. The erect feathered crest on his head went rigid. He puffed out his snow-white feathers in self-defense.

In her normal voice, Blair soothed, "Angel, it's just me. Remember me?"

He fluttered to the swing in the cage, cocked a dark, round eye at her and squawked, "Eck?"

"Just me, Ange," Blair soothed over and over until he calmed. She opened the cage door. Reassured, Angel stepped onto the finger she extended and let her lift him out.

"I'm sorry I scared you, sweetheart." Blair stroked his downy breast and made the noisy kissing sound he loved. He warbled and nuzzled her nose with his closed beak.

"Listen up." She perched Angel on her shoulder while she put the kettle on the stove. "I'll be drawlin' from the time I fly to San Francisco today until I get back. Fred next door will be birdsittin' you for four nights until I return here Friday."

Blair knew it was absurd to talk to a cockatiel. Yet like most bird owners, she had a habit of chatting away to her fine-feathered friend as if he understood every word.

"If Lillian's appendix hadn't burst last week," she went on, "I wouldn't be leavin' you. But she's in the hospital, so *I* have to do the quality-control inspection she was fixin' to start at the St. Martin Hotel today."

Blair groaned. "The St. Martin, of all the cotton-pickin' hotels in the world. Fate is fickle, Ange. If Powers hadn't become resident manager there last month, I wouldn't be goin' to inspect it in this here disguise. After what happened five years ago, darlin' bird, I never want to face him with my own face again."

Angel bobbed his head as if he understood perfectly.

"Stop tweakin' my wig with your beak, Ange." She spooned instant espresso into a cup. "I don't need a reminder that I look funny in this fake getup. Just keep gamblin' like I'm doin' that I won't even catch sight of Powers, much less run into him." She shuddered at the thought. "Thanks for lendin' an ear, Ange. You're a right good little listener, you are."

BLAIR LEFT EARLY ENOUGH for the airport to stop and visit Lillian. She still found it difficult to picture her power-house boss sick.

At fifty-two, Lillian Carroll had more than enough energy to spearhead the hotel evaluation firm she had launched after her husband's death three years earlier. With a combination of personal charm, social connections and bedrock business savvy, she had built up a small firm that evaluated mid-size inns and modest motels at their request and expense. With three evaluators on its payroll, Carroll Management was poised to reel in its first big corporate hotel account.

The Wesmar Hotel Corporation owned the St. Martin in San Francisco and a chain of ten luxury hotels across the country. For years, its own managers had been sent from one hotel to another to examine and report on quality control. The results had been mixed.

Spurred by increasing competition from rival hotel chains, Wesmar was seeking professional, unbiased results from an independent evaluation firm. They wanted to improve all guest services and to determine how pervasive employee theft was—how many bartenders failed to ring up drinks, how many waiters pocketed money from cash customers.

In the hospital elevator, Blair reflected that it made good business sense for her to go to San Francisco in her boss's stead. Carroll Management was keen to compete with larger evaluation firms and was determined to prove itself with an impeccable inspection of the St. Martin. Wesmar could award—or withhold—the lucrative contract for its other ten hotels based on Carroll's performance at the St. Martin.

Scott and Ray, Lillian's two junior evaluators, weren't experienced enough yet to critique a major hotel, so the job had fallen to Blair. Fortunately, Wesmar didn't want any St. Martin employees—including Powers—to know of the evaluation. So Blair was going to the St. Martin as a most discerning and critical undercover guest.

At the door to Lillian's room, she adjusted her glasses, got ready to speak in her thickest southern drawl, and knocked.

"Enter," her boss's throaty voice commanded, "and if it's shots you're selling, make mine a double gin on the rocks."

"Well, shoot," Blair said, walking in, "I'm plumb outta gin. How 'bout a nice mint julep, instead?"

Lillian was propped up in bed. She ran the fingers of one hand through her silvery hair and regarded Blair without a flicker of recognition.

"You have the wrong room, I'm afraid. No mint julep fans here. The Kentucky colonel—minus his gall bladder, poor man—is two doors down."

Blair frowned and moved to the bedside. "Wrong room? They said 309 at the desk, sure's could be."

"Pull up a chair, then, and make yourself comfortable. I'm Lillian Carroll, a lover of good company and conversation, both of which I was missing until you happened by." She held out her hand.

Blair shook it without offering her own name in return. "Pleased to meet you, ma'am." She sat down.

"What part of the deep South do I hear in your fascinating accent?" Lillian inquired, settling back against her pillows.

"New Orleans, ma'am. The Big Easy, they call it."

"Well, fancy that." Lillian smiled. "My most valued employee came here from New Orleans when she was nine years old. She hasn't a trace of the accent left, though." Lillian's cornflower-blue eyes began to gleam. "*The Big Easy.* Now there was a movie I saw more than once. I tell you, I'm still recovering from the scene where Dennis Quaid—"

"Slides his hand right up Ellen Barkin's skirt?" Blair cut in roguishly. "Wasn't that a moment to beat all?"

Lillian nodded, her smile as blissful as Quaid's had been wolfish. "It was. A moment to beat all, by all means."

"Moment enough to beat *this* one, Mrs. Carroll?" Blair reverted to her usual accent. She fluffed her wig and grinned.

"What—?" Lillian gasped, peering at her in astonishment. "*You*, Blair?"

"Me," Blair confirmed. "How's the patient today?"

"Astounded. That's really you in there?"

Blair pushed her thick glasses up from where they had a habit of sliding down her nose. "Just call me *Blah* instead of Blair for the next four days. Am I blah enough that he'll never recognize me?"

Lillian blinked several times. "Not in a trillion years," she marveled. "Blah is quite the word for you, and your accent is an absolute peach. I can't believe my eyes—or ears." She looked Blair up and down with quizzical amazement. "Dear girl, *what* happened between you and Powers D. Knight that you've resorted to this?"

Blair tried not to cringe. "As I said when I first told you the St. Martin had to be your job rather than mine, it's too embarrassing to tell."

"*That* embarrassing, dear?" Lillian inquired gently.

Blair ducked her head, blushing.

"Ah." Lillian regarded her sagely. "So that's what it's all about. I see."

Blair looked up. "See what?"

"Judging from the shade of your cheeks right now, what happened was *romantically* embarrassing."

Blair couldn't hide her surprise that her expression had given her away.

"Were you lovers, Blair?" Lillian asked softly.

Blair's blush deepened. She stared at her hands in her lap and managed the barest of nods.

Lillian let a long moment pass before inquiring in an even gentler tone, "How long, dear?"

"Not long," Blair mumbled, her defenses crumbling under her employer's tolerant, understanding gaze. She looked up and blurted, "It was a one-night mistake—my mistake."

"I've suspected something of the sort from the very first," Lillian soothed with a comforting squeeze of Blair's hand. "My dear, you aren't the only woman to regret a heat-of-the-moment one-night stand. I have an identical regret, myself, in my very distant past. Numerous perfectly nice women do. Live and learn, I always say.

And now that you're in good company, I can easily say there's only one thing that concerns me about your going to the St. Martin."

"What?"

"What if you cross paths with Powers Knight?"

"The odds that we'll cross paths are longer than the odds that it won't rain today in Seattle," Blair replied, glancing at the rain-streaked hospital window. Recovering her poise after her confession, she squared her shoulders. "In the unlikely event that they do cross, there's nothing to give me away. I just proved that I don't look like myself or sound like myself. *And* he knew me before I changed my name."

"Lucky us," said Lillian. "There couldn't have been another Love LaFramboise in the world."

"LaFramboise isn't an unusual name down Louisiana way. Naming girls Love or Lovie isn't unheard of there, either. I was named after my great-grandmother." Blair sighed. "It wasn't a name I could put on a business card in Seattle."

"Do you ever miss your old name, Blair?"

"No, but my parents do. The only way I could keep them from disowning me was to use my father's middle name, Blair, and my mother's maiden name, Sansome. After four years they still haven't quite accepted the change."

"I wish *I* could accept the idea of you going to the St. Martin undercover, dear."

"Don't worry, Lillian. The St. Martin is a twelve-hundred room hotel with a ninety-eight percent occupancy rate this time of year. I'll be just one little brown bee in that busy hive."

"Don't forget Powers lives there," Lillian cautioned. "It's not likely that you'll ever run into the general manager, but unlikely things do happen."

"Unlikely is the key word here," Blair pointed out.

"Blair, if you did run into him . . . what then?"

"Then nothing. How would he guess it's me? Even *you* didn't guess."

"True," Lillian agreed. "This is one clever disguise you've designed. Which is precisely why I hired you. You're clever—and persnickety, too—just like me."

"I'll be both at the St. Martin," Blair promised.

Lillian nodded. "Of course you will. For your sake, I'll pray that he never crosses your path there."

"If he does," Blair said firmly, "he'll walk right by me, none the wiser."

Lillian looked her up and down again. "I daresay he will, unless you keel over at his feet. You do look mousy enough to blend in with the woodwork. And your accent, I repeat, is a peach."

"None the wiser," Blair repeated, nodding.

"Even so, I . . ."

"Don't worry, Lillian."

"I can't help it. I'm twice your age. Fifty-two years have taught me that things happen. Things straight out of thin air. Have you considered what complications could arise should your path and his do more than cross? What if . . . what if they somehow converge?"

"Even if they do, what man looks twice at the generic woman I am?"

"A generic man, perhaps."

"Lillian, nothing about Powers D. Knight is generic. He's taller than average, and he's built like an Olympic swimmer, with a head of thick, wheat-gold hair."

Lillian's eyes widened. "Like Robert Redford's?" As Blair nodded, Lillian murmured, "My word. The best, in other words."

"Close." Blair pictured Powers's unusual russet eyes.

"The best in bed, too?"

"The very b—" Blair caught herself and blushed again.

Lillian chuckled. "Every woman should experience the best and most unforgettable at some point in her life, even if only for one night."

"He'll never look twice at me as I am right now," Blair said. "Not to worry."

"Men are unpredictable creatures, dear girl. If he's as perceptive as he is gorgeous, he could pick up on more than you think. *Is* he perceptive? But why do I ask? No man achieves the status of 'very best' without being perceptive about women, does he?"

Blair shrugged.

"Blair, if the Wesmar account weren't so pivotal, I'd never allow you to take this risk."

"I've taken bigger risks crossing the street, Lillian."

"We *could* still try to postpone the St. Martin job until I'm better," Lillian mused.

Blair shook her head. "Wesmar's shopping for an evaluation firm that delivers what it promises. If we postpone now, you know what will happen."

"I do." Lillian made a face. "We'll never get out of the starting gate. Word will get around to the other hotel chains that we delay, hassle and stall."

"We can't postpone, Lillian."

"You're right, but it doesn't prevent me from fearing something might happen."

"What can happen? My wig's pinned tight enough to weather a tornado. The piece between my teeth can't come out until my dentist unglues it. I look plain, mousy, unexceptional and entirely unworthy of notice. What could happen to me looking like this?"

"Nothing but the unexpected, Blair. If your path does converge somehow with his, and what sparked before sparks again . . . what will you do?"

Raising her eyebrows, perfectly tinted to match her wig, Blair replied in her thickest possible accent, "I'll pour a cold mint julep on it and snuff it out right quick."

THE SOUTHERN DRAWL laid on thick and sickeningly sweet would more than quench any spark, Blair reflected as her flight approached San Francisco.

No sparks would strike, though, she assured herself. A man few woman would overlook, Powers wouldn't look twice at a mousy generic businesswoman.

She closed her eyes, remembering what she had worn on the night she had spent with Powers in her fiancé's bed five years before.

SHE SLIPPED INTO JASON'S apartment in the pitch-black darkness of the most desperate night of her life. She felt her way inside and stripped down to her scanty lace underthings in the living room. A black lace demi-bra and garter belt. Seamed stockings. Stiletto heels. She was determined to be totally outrageous for Jason. Shivering, she located a glass and the cognac in Jason's liquor cabinet—stone sober, she could *never* be the naughty, fun femme fatale that she intended to be tonight.

She sat in his favorite armchair and tipped his fine brandy, imbibing just enough to lighten her head and frizz her senses. Just enough to blur the line between reality and fantasy. Just enough to stop feeling ridiculously raunchy, and start feeling scandalously seductive. Not like the woman Jason knew, but like a shameless sexcapade in black lace.

She shed her inhibitions with each sip, recalling scattered images from the *Kama Sutra* she had checked out of the library and the adult video she had rented to prepare herself. Then she felt her way in the dreamlike darkness to Jason's bed and the man sleeping in it.

"It's me, loverman," she murmured, kissing him half awake, "but not the me you know. Tonight I'm the loverwoman in every dream you've ever had." She knelt on the bed, straddled his hips, and ran her palms from his shoulders down to his hands.

"Who . . . ?" he drowsily whispered.

"Not a word," she softly commanded against his lips. "Don't speak. Don't think. Just *feel* who I am tonight especially for you."

She silenced him with a kiss and guided his fingers with hers, tracing the line of her throat down to the tender hollow where her pulse throbbed.

"But, who . . . ?" he whispered a second time.

"Let's just say a friend sent me," she replied.

"Who?"

"Stifle it, loverman." Tunneling the fingers of one hand in his hair, she led his hand slowly down her body with the other. "I'm in control tonight," she boldly reproved. "I do the talking or I'll leave. You don't want me to leave just yet . . . do you?"

She felt the slow, dreamy shake of his head against her palm. Strange, she thought fuzzily, how thick his hair felt. Caught up in the fantasy, feeling the cognac flowing warm in her blood, flooded with sensation, she dismissed the thought to marvel at how altered *everything* seemed. The bed felt smaller, the room larger, the hour later, the air thinner, the sheets silkier, the man between them heavier, stronger, harder.

Blair heard his sharp intake of breath when she led his fingers to trace the lacy contours of her bra, his sharper breath when she guided his touch down to her garter belt, his helpless groan of desire as his palms traveled the lengthy back seams of her stockings.

He lost his cool over her garter-clasps, tracing the tops of her stockings and sucking in ragged breaths. He was coming awake with passion as he had done in bed before their engagement, as he had failed to do in the three months since then. Jason—and her desire for him—had driven her, clad only in black lace, to his bed. Jason, her first and only lover.

"Feel me," she urged with a feline growl, pressing his warm palms to cup the twin curves of her bare bottom. "Dream me tonight, loverman. Want me. You *do* want me, don't you?" She relented, then. "I'll grant you one word. Yes? Or no?"

"Yes." His strangled whisper echoed in the darkness. His fingers roamed the length of her legs again, then moved upward between her thighs. He felt her lacy thong bikini and groaned. He slipped his fingers under it to stroke her. Intimately. How different his touch felt, she dimly thought.

It had been so long since Jason had made love to her, though. Strained, celibate months in which she'd despaired that he'd ever touch her again with sexual desire. Perhaps her memories of his loving touch were blurred with time . . . and cognac.

Or perhaps, she thought, he had never touched her quite this way because she had never played to his—or her own—lustiest fantasies. She had never worn x-rated lingerie to bed or whispered uncensored words and phrases in his ear before. It hadn't been necessary before their engagement, for Jason had been easily aroused. Since then, he had been impotent.

Tonight, however, there was no shortage of erect manhood between Jason's bedsheets. And no shortage of sexual prowess, either. She rubbed her lace-covered breasts against his chest. He stroked her with his fingers, then raised his head toward hers and stroked her lips with his tongue. He drew her down and kissed her, his tongue swirling around hers, teasing, tasting, tantalizing.

He'd never kissed her like that before, she hazily thought. Nor had he ever opened the clasp of her bra with a flick of his wrist as he did now. And then he proceeded to please her in ways he'd never pleased her before.

BLAIR OPENED HER EYES reluctantly.

How had she not had a glimmer right then?

Every day for the past five years, Blair had asked herself that question and many others. How could she have been bared with such expert speed, without suspecting in the first moments that the man in Jason's bed wasn't Jason?

How had she proceeded to make love with that man without even one moment of mental clarity in that cognac-and-fantasy-flushed night? The man in Jason's bed had been bigger by enough to make a difference, hungrier, more eager to give her all she could take.

Had she truly believed that the provocative seductress she had made herself into had regenerated Jason to such an awesome extent? Or had she simply been so desperately in love that she had needed to believe she could cure him?

Now, older and wiser at twenty-seven, she knew what Jason's problem had been. Fear of commitment. He'd gotten icy-cold feet when he'd promised to marry her, and tried to conceal his relief when she ended their engagement after that fateful night.

Blair felt a tap on her arm. "Ma'am?" a male voice intruded on her thoughts.

She focused on the flight steward who hovered over her reclined aisle seat.

"What is it?"

"Please fasten your safety belt and bring your seat upright," he said. "We're preparing to land."

Blair obeyed the steward and glanced across the empty middle seat at the passenger next to the window. She smiled at the seventy-year-old man with whom she had chatted during the first half of the trip.

He wore his age extremely well. His full head of hair and trim beard were white, his eyes a warm brown, his suit a muted navy pinstripe with a blue bachelor-button in the lapel. A perfect gentleman, he had offered to exchange seats at the beginning of the flight. She had declined his offer, charmed by his courtly manner.

In their idle conversation together, she had learned he was a retired realtor from British Columbia, a widower with six grandchildren. He was traveling to visit his son who had recently been transferred to San Francisco. Blair had revealed little of herself aside from the basic purpose of her trip. "Business," she had told him, and he had politely refrained from inquiring what that might be.

"Have you had a nice nap?" he asked.

"Er, yes. Very refreshing." A blush tinged her cheeks. Black-lace scenes had filled her mind during her so-called nap.

"Excuse me?" He leaned toward her and touched his finger to his hearing aid.

Blair caught the slip in her accent and covered the error quickly. "Very refreshin', thank you."

"I believe I'll catch twenty winks, myself, after I reach the hotel," he remarked, settling back. "I hope the room my son booked for me is quiet."

"You're not stayin' over with kin, sir?"

"On the contrary, I am," he replied. "He lives there, you see, in the hotel. I'll be just a few doors down from his suite, I believe he said."

It was a comment that caused Blair a moment of anxiety. She calmed herself with the knowledge that San Francisco was full of residence hotels.

"Be seein' a few of your gran'kids, will you?" she continued.

"Oh, no. It's my two older sons who have six children between them. The son I'm visiting is still single." He glanced out the window at the city below and back at Blair. "In my opinion he's been single too long. He swears his work doesn't leave him time for romance. *I* say, what's life without romance in it?"

"Me, too," Blair agreed. "Not that I have oodles of romance in mine, mind you."

"Well, you should," he said thoughtfully. "Every young woman should."

"Us plain ones miss out mostly," Blair returned. "It's a fact of life." Even reasonably attractive women missed out, Blair thought. Herself, for instance, in the past few years.

"I wouldn't call you plain," he protested.

"I would, and it's the honest truth. I'm no ravin' beauty or romance novel heroine, and I know it."

The man in the window seat shook his head. "Looks may be paramount to some men, but not for me. My beloved wife was no raving beauty. Pleasant-looking, my parents said when I brought her home for dinner. But beneath that pleasant exterior, she was ravishing. Just as I—" he paused to scrutinize her, then resumed "—just as I suspect *you* are beneath your own pleasant surface, young woman."

Flustered, Blair brushed at her sleeve. "You're so smooth and charmin' that you could pass for a southern gentleman easy as pecan pie."

"Perceptive is the word," he corrected her. "If my son brought someone like you home for my approval, I'd approve at once." His gaze probed hers. "Please don't think I'm flirting. Would you think me presumptuous if I asked your permission to introduce you to him while you're in the city?"

"Presumptuous?" Blair gulped. "Not at all. But—see— I'll be so terrible busy with business that I won't have a minute to spare."

He looked rueful. "I'm not cut out to play matchmaker, it seems. Busy young people have more modern devices than formal introductions for getting together, I'm sure."

"Like the personals, you mean?"

"Like the personals," he agreed with mild distaste. "I suppose they serve a purpose. I really should never have suggested what I did. I thought my son would find your accent as delightful as I find it, and I thought perhaps you'd appreciate his winning smile. It was simply senility, I suspect. Besides, as they so unromantically put things these days, you're both 'geographically undesirable' for each other, aren't you?"

"Very," Blair agreed, relieved to have squirmed off the blind-date hook.

"Oh, well. It was worth a try. You can understand that, as his father, I'd like to see him married and happy in his personal life. Career-wise, he couldn't be happier. I'm glad of that."

"What business is he in, by the by?"

"Hotel management."

"Oh." Nothing to tense up about, Blair told herself firmly.

"He's risen fast to have become the youngest top manager in the company."

"Oh?" She tensed slightly.

"Indeed. He was promoted to resident general manager a month ago," came the reply, accompanied by a smile of fatherly pride. "He was transferred recently from Chicago."

Blair felt suddenly short of breath. She forced herself to inhale deeply, then asked, "To what hotel?"

"The St. Martin, downtown."

Blair stopped breathing. She remembered Lillian cautioning, "Things happen . . ." and "What if . . . ?"

"And where are *you* staying while you're here?" Powers Knight's father inquired as the plane touched down.

2

STRIDING THROUGH the arcade of airport shops on the way to meet his father's plane, Powers Knight checked his watch. With several minutes to spare before passengers deplaned, he asked himself why the big rush. The answer was habit. A devil of a habit to break.

After five straight years of working overtime in overdrive, slowing down even a little was no easy thing to do. His doctor had sternly prescribed a change of pace a week ago after a physical, otherwise Powers would never have considered it.

"Time out," he muttered, forcibly braking his swift stride to a stroll. Following doctor's orders was damned difficult, he stewed as he made himself saunter past restaurants, newsstands and retail shops. He'd have sped past them last week.

"You're a classic case of all work and no play," the doctor had pronounced. "Symptomatic tight chest, elevated blood pressure and shortness of breath. Keep it up and you'll be a classic Type A."

"What's the prescription?" Powers had asked.

"To begin with, one long, do-nothing vacation."

Powers had shaken his head immediately. "No vacations, no way. I have a hotel to manage."

The doctor had raised his eyebrows. "You have a hotel that's managing *you*, young man, from the symptoms you exhibit. Keep burning the candle at both ends and you'll be prime for a stress coronary before you know it."

"Anything but a vacation, Doc. Give me an alternative."

"The alternative is to pull back and do less. Delegate. Walk, don't run. Take five. Linger a while. Lighten up. Easy does it. Hold your horses. See me in two weeks for a progress check."

Next to a vacation, a general slowdown had been the last thing Powers had wanted to hear about.

"It's that or rush through life with a ticking time bomb in that tight chest of yours," the doctor had warned. "If you want to breathe deeply again, kick back and smell the roses."

Recalling that grim warning, Powers tried to take a really deep breath—without success. He slowed his pace and tried again. No go. He came to a halt and made a third unsuccessful attempt. Damn. He loosened his tie and moved on at an even slower place than before, a pace that rubbed against the grain with every step.

"Smell the roses," he muttered irritably. He looked around for a flower stand, tempted to pin a bud on his lapel. He checked his watch again. A snail's pace, he reflected glumly, was not his style. In no time at all, his effort to locomote like a tortoise instead of a hare had become one big bore. Frustrated, he began noticing things he'd never noticed in an airport before.

The shop windows that lined the way to the arrival gates were not the blur they had always been in his previous haste. He found himself looking closely into them as he passed. It was the only way to distract himself from the extremely difficult task of holding his horses to a plodding walk.

Passing a bookstore window, he was struck by the staggering number of titles on display, and remembered that he hadn't read a book in ages. Reading for pleasure was another prescription the doctor had ordered.

Trudging on, he passed a jewelry store window displaying diamond engagement rings. His father wished that he'd fall in love, marry and settle down. Even the doctor had said, "Find someone to come home to and you'll *want* to leave work after eight hours."

He came to a lingerie shop window. The display of intimate black lace dainties gave him the first agreeable reason to heed medical advice and linger a while. There were slinky negligees and seductive camisoles cut up to here and down to there. Leaving as little as possible to the imagination were saucy brassieres, sassy tap pants, seamed silk stockings, and a pair of see-through bikini panties with a blooming red rose embroidered on the strategic front triangle.

His eyes settled on a garter belt that featured a tiny red satin rosebud on each of its four frilled stocking clasps. He slid his tongue over his lips. Had there been rosebuds on that wisp of black lace five years ago? He had awakened the morning after and found a black silk stocking draped over the lampshade, its mate, still clipped to the garter belt, draped over the headboard of Jason Aldren's bed. Sheer silk and black lace, yes, but no red satin rosebuds.

What a night! It had been the supreme peak of his sexual experience. He breathed deeply and let the breath out in a long sigh. Unforgettable. Powers breathed all the way in again, and realized the feat he had just accomplished. It was the deepest he'd filled his lungs with air in a long time, possibly since waking up so long ago with the woman of every one of his fantasies in his arms.

Maybe the solution wasn't in slowing down at all, he mused, staring into the window again. Maybe he did need a woman in his life. A woman in black lace who would wake him at midnight and whisper, "Dream me tonight, loverman." A fantasy loverwoman unlike any other.

Love LaFramboise, in short. He grimaced and turned from the provocative items in the window. Love had unknowingly led him into the hotel career he prized. She had also ruined him for every other woman. Black lace never failed to remind him of her, a woman he'd never forget.

She had been the only woman to ever fulfill his fondest fantasies, the only woman to tempt forth his most powerful response. Though her approach had been as bold as brass, there had been a freshness to it, and a surprising shyness had sweetened every randy word she had uttered. Though patently provocative, her seduction had not been practised or professional. Yet she had aroused every male instinct he possessed.

She had given all of herself to him, both bodily and emotionally. He'd never forget how generous, unselfish and achingly vulnerable she had been. Because of that, for long, wild moments he had thought of begging her to be his woman for life. His instincts for finding the paradoxical qualities he needed in a mate had been unerring when he'd found Love.

Unnerved by that thought, Powers reverted to his habitual behavior and checked his watch. He scowled. Where had the time gone? If he didn't hustle, he'd be late.

He reached the gate, chest tight and short of breath again, just as the first in a long stream of passengers came off the Seattle flight. His father wasn't among them. It would be just like him to be the last to deplane. Matthew Knight was a classic Type-B personality.

Powers had never known Matthew to be hurried, driven or uptight. He'd never seen him fidget, drum his fingers or overwork. Patient, good-natured, easygoing, that was his father. Competitive, hard-driving, short-scheduled, that was himself.

Powers had thought of himself as more fortunate and successful than his father had ever been. After his visit to the doctor, faced with the fact that success had a price he wasn't eager to pay, he was looking forward to his father's visit more than ever. He hoped to learn something—like how to smell the roses.

Powers shoved his hands in his pants pockets and shifted in place from heel to toe, foot to foot. He checked off his plans for Matthew's week-long visit. Dinner with him in the St. Martin's poshest dining room tonight.

Lunch in Chinatown, breakfast at Fisherman's Wharf, nine holes of golf, an Alcatraz tour, Golden Gate Park, Grace Cathedral . . .

The trickle of passengers dwindled to none. He walked over and peered down the long, empty exit ramp. Then he checked the time and date on his watch. As casual as his father might be, it was hard for Powers to imagine him getting the day or time wrong, or missing the flight altogether. He stared at his watch, then tapped the crystal face of it with his finger. Had the battery in it gone dead or something?

"Searching for *me* in there, son?"

Powers looked up and saw Matthew coming down the ramp with a woman by his side. She was, he saw in an instant, quite plain, nothing special in the way of looks. Superb ankles, though. He noted her chunky suit and clunky shoes. She blushed behind the enormous glasses that covered most of her face. His father was probably the first eligible male ever to pay her a moment's attention.

"How you doing, Pop?" Powers said, smiling, thinking that his father was a shining example of their old English surname. What other man would have even noticed this unremarkable female, much less been knightly enough to escort her as if she were beauty incarnate?

Matthew beamed, "I'm splendid, son, splendid." He patted the woman's left hand, which was tucked in the crook of his elbow, and turned to her. "My boy and I are the demonstrative sort. Would you excuse us for a moment before I introduce you?"

"Y'all go right ahead," she replied, untucking her hand.

There was no ring on her ring finger, and Powers knew a grits 'n' gravy drawl paired with plainness could be more a liability than an asset outside of the South. He felt a tender wince of sympathy for her. He hid it in the hearty, backslapping embrace he shared with his father.

Blair couldn't help admiring their obvious affection for each other. At the same time, she felt like an animal caught in a snare that would tighten with her feeblest attempt at escape.

While they had waited for the other passengers to deplane, Matthew had asked where she'd be lodging in San Francisco. "I'm stayin' at the St. Martin, too," she had replied truthfully, knowing she might run into him in an elevator or restaurant there.

"You're riding there from the airport with me and Powers in the hotel limousine, then," he had declared. "Allow me to introduce myself. Matthew Knight, at your service. If you don't mind addressing me by my first name, I'll feel much less ancient than I am."

There had been nothing else for her to do but shake the hand he had offered.

Now Blair gripped the handle of her briefcase and watched Matthew and Powers embrace. She couldn't help noticing that Powers was everything she had remembered.

Five years hadn't tarnished the rich gold of his hair or diminished its thickness and slight wave. Dressed in a dark business suit, he appeared as lean and solid as he had felt that night and looked the next morning. His smile was as striking, his teeth were as straight and white, his squint lines only a trifle deeper.

All in all, he was a most magnificent man. What a magnificent lover he had been, as well. Powers and Matthew turned to her.

"Miss Blair Sansome from Seattle," Matthew said, pulling her forward, "my son Powers."

"So pleased t'meet you, Powers." She forced her hand to move, a hand that had caressed every inch of his body countless times one dark night.

"I'm very pleased to meet *you*, Miss Sansome," Powers said, taking her hand and finding it as cold as if she'd alighted from an iceberg instead of a 737. *Poor woman*, he thought again as she slid her hand away. There were her superb ankles, however, he reminded himself. And a flawless complexion, he noted. As he looked at her, she ducked her head. *Shy, too. No black lace garters in Miss Sansome's lingerie drawer.*

"Guess what?" Matthew said smiling broadly. "Blair has reservations for four nights at the St. Martin. I invited her to ride in with us, if you don't mind."

"Not at all." Powers glanced at his father. Was Matthew hatching ideas—cozy little fix-up ideas, in relation to this very plain, unmarried young woman and his very unmarried youngest son? Powers hoped not. He had enough to juggle with the executive management of a luxury hotel, his father's visit and too many Type-A symptoms.

"Let's head down to baggage claim," he said. "The limo's at the curb there. Fritz is at the wheel."

"Fritz," Matthew repeated with relish. He offered his arm. "Fine name for a chauffeur, don't you think, Blair?"

"Fine it is," Blair replied through stiff lips. She could still feel the thrill that had swirled up her arm and spread through her body at the touch of Powers's hand. The same powerful hand that had known her in every intimate detail that dark night.

It was going to be a long ride.

FRITZ HAD JUST GUIDED the long white limo onto Highway 101 when every northbound lane of traffic slowed down and ground to a halt.

"Looks like a fender-bender ahead," he advised.

Powers glanced impatiently at his watch. "Just what we need."

"Ain't it the truth," Blair murmured. Sitting between Powers and Matthew, she closed her eyes in disbelief at the unwelcome delay. Given the way her flight had turned out, heaven only knew how long this fateful day might last.

"Well, now, it's a sunny, lovely April day." Matthew pointed out cheerfully. "Who would believe that I flew out of Vancouver in snow flurries, or that Blair boarded in Seattle in a driving rainstorm?"

Blair opened her eyes, stared at the back of Fritz's chauffeur's cap, and politely replied, "No one in these parts, I expect. This here surely is the Golden State."

"Give me sunshine over snow and rain any day—" Powers drummed the fingers of both hands on his thighs "—though traffic couldn't be worse right now if there was a blizzard blowing."

Matthew smiled. "More time for all of us to enjoy the day—and for us gentlemen, in particular, to enjoy more of this lady's company. Which part of the South are you from, Blair?"

"New Orleans."

"I have an old college friend whose fiancée was from there," Powers commented. He abruptly looked out of the window. "Remember Jason Aldren, Pop?"

Blair kept her eyes on Fritz's cap, her hands tightly clasped in her lap. What had ever possessed Jason to share that inconsequential bit of history with Powers?

"Jason Aldren," Matthew mused. "Your swim-team buddy?"

"Yep. Remember him?"

"Now that you mention him, yes." Matthew nodded. "You two were always playing tricks on each other. And you traded clothes all the time, if I recall correctly. What ever became of Jason?"

Powers straighted his tie. "Last I heard, his engagement had broken up and he'd moved to Toronto. He had a habit of getting engaged and wishing the next day that he hadn't. His Seattle fiancée was his third or fourth . . . I don't remember which."

Blair's eyes widened. *Third or fourth? Since when?* She struggled to conceal her shock.

"An unfortunate habit," Matthew observed.

"Very unfortunate," Powers agreed, still looking out the window. "I met her in Seattle . . . black hair, green eyes . . . far too good for Jason."

Matthew frowned. "I didn't know you'd ever been in Seattle, Powers."

"That's because I hitchhiked there from grad school without telling you," he admitted, glancing at Matthew. "I knew you wouldn't approve."

"Hitchhiked? I certainly *would* have disapproved. You had a car then. Why didn't you drive?"

"Because the transmission was acting up and I was temporarily short of funds and . . ."

"And you hated to wait, as usual," Matthew supplied. "You were as impatient then as you are now."

"Impulsive, Pop. I was between semesters and needed a break after finals. Just before my final semester of grad school, I got the bright idea that I had to see my old swim-buddy for old times' sake. When I got to Seattle, he was getting cold feet on his engagement and he was hot to drive down to a house party in California. With school starting in two days, there was no way I could—" He broke off and looked at Blair, then at Matthew. "Let's talk old times and friends later. This can't be of any great interest to Blair."

Blair had never managed to pry out of Jason where he had been on that fateful night. She protested quickly, "Oh, but it's most interestin' and all. I'm glued. Please go on."

Powers shrugged and continued, "I couldn't get down to California and back in time for school, but Jason went.

Said he wanted to break off with his fiancée, but had to get away for a few days to work up the courage. So I spent the night at his place and hitched back to school the next day."

"His poor fiancée," said Matthew. "Did you meet her before or after you found out that Jason intended to jilt her?"

Blair sat still and straight, frozen in place.

Powers ran his finger around the inside of his collar and cleared his throat. "After."

"Hmm. That couldn't have been comfortable for you, knowing what was in store for her."

"Well . . . knowing she was too good for him helped a bit."

"Poor girl." Matthew shook his head. "I hope her heart wasn't too badly broken."

"Oh, I imagine it was for a time there," Blair dared to comment, and felt indignant enough to say, "Might be you should have clued her in to his bad habits."

Powers mulled that over for a moment before replying, "Swim-team buddies don't rat on each other. It was Jason's place to clue her in, not mine."

"Poor girl," she murmured, echoing Matthew.

"No woman that beautiful would have had to suffer alone very long," Powers said. He shifted in his seat. "If he hadn't been an old pal, I'd have looked her up myself."

Blair almost choked.

"But he was a pal, and I didn't," Powers went on. "A semester later, when I finished grad school, I was hired by Wesmar as a management trainee in Miami. Wrong time, wrong place."

"Ah, well." Matthew sighed and looked hopefully from Blair to Powers. "There's a time and place for everything, they say."

"Fasten your seat belts. Here we go again," Fritz announced. The limo inched forward.

Blair breathed a silent sigh of relief. With any luck she would soon be in her hotel room behind a double-locked door. She would rip off her itchy wig and then she would sit down and hatch a plot to avoid Powers and Matthew like the plague. Last, she would pray that nothing else would happen in San Francisco.

What could be worse, though, than the fix she was in?

Nothing, she decided—and crossed her fingers.

3

CROSSED FINGERS DIDN'T DO the trick. By the time she spotted the St. Martin up ahead, Blair was trying to cross her toes as well.

"Have you dinner plans for tonight, Blair?" Matthew had just asked, right after he had somehow made it impossible for her to decline his invitation to join him and Powers for cocktails.

"I'm afraid I do have plans," she replied. Though dinner in her room hadn't been part of her original plans for the night, it was definitely featured now.

"Another night, perhaps? We'd be pleased if you'd join us," Matthew encouraged. "Wouldn't we, son?"

"Our pleasure," Powers concurred, meaning it. He'd discovered he liked Miss Blair Sansome and wouldn't mind seeing more of her. Or more correctly, hearing more of her. In light of the slowdown his doctor had prescribed, she and her southern drawl couldn't have happened along at a better time.

During the protracted ride, he had become aware that her drawn-out speech pattern had a surprisingly beneficial effect. It relaxed him. As he had talked with her and Matthew, he felt his inner gears downshift. Blair's languid, lilting vowels and lazy pace had eventually set him to thinking of porch swings and long afternoons, balmy bayous and moonlit magnolias. Not once had his thoughts turned, as they usually did, to work.

"Oh, I'd love to join you-all, but business is business and I have appointments and client dinners comin' out my ears." Blair crossed her legs and then nervously re-crossed them.

Her skirt shifted and Powers caught sight of the length of her calf and curve of her knee. He almost gawked. More than her ankles were superb. A leg-man to the core, he covertly savored the discovery, concluding that if she was perfect from ankles to knees, her thighs couldn't be far behind.

Then she shoved her skirt back down to mid-calf and left him wondering why a woman with stunning legs hid them away, and why she obscured her lucent complexion and delicate profile with thick, oversize glasses. As for her no-style hairstyle, she'd look much more attractive with it cut short and feathered—as Love La-Framboise had worn hers.

Love again. His habit of comparing every woman he met to Love had gone from bad to worse. It was as ingrained as the habit of drumming his fingers on his knee, he realized, and forced the rhythm to a halt. He had less success in halting the comparison. From what he'd seen of Blair's legs, they were probably equal to Love's. And considering her tranquilizing accent, charming southernisms, translucent skin, and gorgeous legs, he was disappointed she wouldn't be at the St. Martin longer than four nights. He wondered if she'd go out with him.

"Finally," she sighed. Powers looked up and discovered with surprise that they'd arrived at the canopied entrance to the hotel. He was breathing deeply without effort, too. It occurred to him then that the lace window display at the airport had induced his first deep breaths that day. Miss Blair Sansome had brought on some more. The more he thought about it, the better she looked.

A uniformed doorman led Blair, Powers and Matthew through a revolving glass door into the stately lobby of the St. Martin. As they approached the long marble registration desk, Blair hoped that nothing more would go wrong.

"Miss Blair Sansome and Matthew Knight checking in," Powers said to the desk clerk who entered the information into a computer. Blair couldn't see the screen.

Please, she prayed, *please, no hang-ups, foul-ups, mix-ups.* The instant the young man frowned, she knew heaven had more in store for her than a simple answer to a prayer.

Powers leaned over the desk. "Problem, Jay?"

"Yes, but it's nothing that wouldn't be solved by a suite for one night and a move tomorrow morning at Miss Sansome's convenience."

Blair knew from experience what that meant. The St. Martin had either overbooked on the medium-priced room she had reserved or it'd had more stay-overs than anticipated. Though there might be lower-priced rooms available, a luxury hotel like the St. Martin would try not to downgrade her to a standard room. An upgrade to a suite at the rate quoted on her reservation was a bargain and made a move the next morning seem less inconvenient.

"A suite will be charmin' for one night," she assured Jay. "I'll be pleased as punch to move tomorrow mornin'."

"Thank you for understanding, ma'am."

Jay handed her a registration form and a pen. She signed and returned the form to him with her credit card for reference.

"Which suite is that, Jay?" Powers asked.

"The Golden Gateway on your floor, sir."

"Is it reserved any time over the next four days?"

Jay checked the computer screen. "Not until late next week, Mr. Knight."

"In that case, please make a note that Miss Sansome will complete her stay in the Golden Gateway at the lower rate."

"Yes, sir." Jay returned her credit card.

"But it's fine as fine can be with me to move tomorrow," Blair protested.

Powers turned to her and smiled. "A St. Martin guest with business appointments and client dinners one after the other doesn't need the hassle of an unnecessary move."

"But—"

He held up a hand. "Enjoy the suite at the room rate you reserved, compliments of the management."

"But—"

"Indulge him, Blair," Matthew urged with a twinkle in his eye. "He's not a man to argue with unless you have time to waste, and what busy businesswoman has time like that on her hands?"

"But—"

"Good work, Jay," Powers cut in, taking the two keys Jay handed him. "I'll show my father and the lady to their quarters since we're all on the same floor. Send the next available bellman with our bags, please."

Aware that further protest—or prayer—would be futile, Blair braced herself for the journey to her suite. It proceeded without a hitch until Matthew stopped and snapped his fingers just as they reached the elevators.

"Pardon me while I backtrack," he said. "I forgot to pack something, but I'm certain I can purchase it in the lobby gift shop. You two run along. I'll be up shortly."

Powers tossed him the key. "Twenty-seventh floor, Pop. Turn left when you get off the elevator."

At that moment, Blair could think of few things worse than being alone in an elevator with Powers Knight. *Let it fill up with lots of people,* she silently offered in a last hope that at least one prayer might be granted.

Like every other entreaty she had sent up since leaving Seattle, it bombed. Alone in the leather-padded cubicle with Powers, she gripped the handle of her briefcase tightly and watched the double doors close her in with him. She fixed her gaze on the carpeted floor.

"Thank you kindly for your kindness with the limo and the suite," she began, "but—"

"You're very welcome, Blair," Powers interjected. "It's my greatest pleasure to make—and keep—a guest happy."

Blair stifled a frustrated sigh.

"So you're here on business," Powers remarked as their ascent began.

"I surely am. Strictly business."

"Ever been to San Francisco before?"

She shook her head.

"I hadn't, either, until a month ago," he volunteered. "I haven't seen a lot of the city yet, I'm ashamed to say. Now that Pop's visiting, I have the good excuse I need." He paused. "Think you'll be sight-seeing much?"

She shook her head again.

"Too bad. The weather's perfect. The fog's clearing before noon most days."

Blair acknowledged his weather report with a nod and switched her briefcase to her other hand—the one next to Powers. It would provide the barrier she needed between herself and his vital presence.

He stood close enough that she could smell the spicy scent of his after-shave. Close enough that she could feel heat radiating from his body. She swallowed hard, remembering the body heat he had generated in Jason's bed, then raised her gaze for a quick assessment of his expression. She found him assessing hers.

"You wouldn't happen to be related to anyone in Seattle, would you?" he inquired, looking sheepish at being caught staring.

"Oh, no," she lied. "My kin are all down South." She touched her tongue to her lips and risked inquiring, "What makes you ask?"

"I don't know." He shrugged, looking puzzled. "Something about you reminds me of . . . someone. . . ."

Blair felt as if her stomach had fallen all the way back down to the lobby. "If you've ever been south," she ventured, "it's most likely my accent that's strikin' your chord."

He shrugged again and looked away. "Could be. I was there overnight at a sales meeting last year. What led you to leave New Orleans for Seattle?"

"A job," she replied, which was true. The accounting firm her father worked for had transferred him permanently from Louisiana to Seattle. She watched each floor number on the control panel light up as the elevator continued its unhurried ascent. Eight. Nine. Ten. Blair made a mental note to give the St. Martin's elevator system the lowest rating possible for its lack of speed. Eleven. Twelve.

On the fourteenth floor, it stopped. Blair was relieved at the prospect of being joined by more passengers. When the door didn't open, she glanced at Powers.

He punched a red button on the panel. Nothing happened. He punched it several times. Nothing.

"Damn," he swore under his breath. "Not again."

Blair stepped back against the rear wall of the elevator. "You wouldn't be sayin' we're stuck, would you?"

"I wish I could say no, but one of the other elevators jammed like this last week," he said, jabbing the button repeatedly. "It must be as catching as a cold. Or maybe the thirteenth floor's bad luck no matter what number a hotel gives it in deference to superstition."

Blair closed her eyes and remembered Lillian's qualms. *Things happen.* "This happen very often?" she murmured.

"Once every half century until last week, according to the hotel engineer," Powers replied. "Don't worry. A silent alarm went off right away in his office. He'll call the repair company. We'll be out before you know it." He checked his watch.

Blair opened her eyes. "How long might that be?"

"Twenty minutes or so if last week's anything to go by."

Twenty minutes. Alone. In an elevator. With Powers Knight.

He blew out an apologetic breath. "I'm sorry for your inconvenience, but things happen in hotels at the damnedest times. Here," he offered, pulling off his suit jacket, "have a seat, compliments of the management." Executing a swift knee-bend, he laid the garment lining-up on the carpeted floor.

Blair stared as Powers smoothed the gray silk with his strong hands. Before she could move away, he clasped her hand and tugged gently.

"Have a seat," he repeated.

"But where will you . . . ?"

"I'll rough it." He took her briefcase from her and set it on the floor. "It's the least I can do to maintain the St. Mart's reputation for superlative service come hell, high water or stuck elevators."

"But . . ."

"But? I'm beginning to think that's the only word you know, Blair. But *what?*"

"Nothin'. Thank you so much." She knelt on his jacket. The silk was warm, so warm from his body. She sank down until she was seated with her legs tucked under her skirt and her back against the rear wall.

Powers settled at her side, his shoulder touching hers. He stretched his legs out full length and crossed them at the ankles.

"There," he said. "Comfortable?"

"Very." Again he was too close. And he hadn't let go of her hand.

He squeezed her hand slightly and said teasingly, "Brr. What icy fear do I feel in your hand, Blair? Afraid you won't get out of this alive?"

"P'rhaps," she responded, worrying more about what his touch was doing to her than getting out alive. For one thing, it was making her want more of what she had experienced with him before. It was also making her wish she had never seen him until today, for he was a single man few single woman would mind getting better acquainted with in a stuck elevator. He was a man a woman could imagine falling in love with at first sight. Or first touch.

"Relax and warm up," he said, lacing his fingers through hers, thinking it was ironic for a Type A to be urging anyone to relax. "The six guests who got stuck in one of these last week got out without a hitch. So will we. In the meantime, tell me what business brings you to San Francisco."

"Oh, I'm a—a CPA," she improvised quickly. It was a profession she knew something about, thanks to her father. Not a lot, but enough to slip past a nonaccountant.

Powers nodded. "Tax or audit?"

Blair knew if he was making that distinction at the outset, she'd have to improvise quicker than ever. He was waiting for her answer. She bit her lip. What *was* that little-known branch of accounting her father had once mentioned? Some kind of legal something or other. It came to her just as Powers's eyebrows began to rise at her hesitation.

"Litigation support."

His eyebrows leveled out and he shook his head. "Never heard of it. Sounds . . . interesting."

"Very interestin'," she agreed, "but terribly technical. Not at all excitin' to anyone but us litigation supporters, for sure. This hotel business, on the other hand, now here's excitement galore with elevators stuck on the thirteenth floor and all. How'd you get to be manager here?"

Powers pondered the question for a moment before he replied, "Too much hard work and no play is how I got where I am, if my doctor's right. I knew I was a workaholic, but I didn't know I was a potential Type A."

"Oh?" Blair said to keep him talking.

"Yeah. Anything I can do to slow down, I'm supposed to do whenever I can." He cracked a dry smile. "Guess what a marooned workaholic would be doing right now in an elevator if you weren't here to keep his mind off work?"

"Spinnin' his wheels to get back to work, I reckon."

"You reckon right. It's a good thing you were along on this ride to keep me occupied."

Blair fervently wished she could say the same. Instead, she said, "Your daddy'll be worryin' his mind about us."

"No, he won't." Powers spoke with certainty. "By the time my daddy discovers he should have been worryin' his mind about us, he'll be as friendly with the newsstand clerk, the florist, the bell captain, the concierge and the coffee shop hostess as he is with you." He paused for breath. "And I'm not criticizing. I only wish I had inherited half his knack of smelling the roses along the way. What do they call it down south—smelling the magnolias?"

How, Blair wondered distractedly, was she going to get her hand back? Powers was rubbing his thumb back and forth along hers.

"Magnolias. Y-yes," she stammered, then tossed the ball back in his court. "Your daddy did mention you're not in the habit of lettin' grass grow under your feet."

Powers rolled his eyes. "He would say that. What else did he mention in regard to me?"

"That he was proud of all you've accomplished." She'd never known that a hand could heat up so fast. It seemed a lifetime ago that she'd felt certain she'd never cross paths with Powers Knight. And it seemed it was only last night that he'd done to every inch of her body what he was doing right now to her hand.

"He'd be prouder if I'd get married and settle down, believe me," Powers retorted mildly, "but that's as unlikely as it's ever been. Or did he mention that, too?"

"He did speak a word to that effect, yes."

Powers chuckled. "I'm not surprised. I wouldn't be surprised, either, if he spoke about that to a single woman like you for a specific reason." He paused for a heartbeat. "Or are you married? Pop didn't introduce you as 'Miss' by mistake, did he?"

"Me?" Blair remembered telling Matthew she was single. "Oh—why, no. No mistakin' what I am." She pushed her glasses up to the bridge of her nose with her free hand, wishing she could push back a few other things that were slipping in the wrong direction. Her libido, to begin with. And his eyes. He kept studying her face, looking puzzled by what he saw one minute, intrigued the next.

"Have you ever been married, Blair?"

"Me? Uh—no."

"Engaged?"

"Once upon a time, I was, but that spark never quite caught fire."

At that, Powers smiled full-strength, looking straight into her eyes. "You know, the way you say things—'Ah' for I, 'quaht' for quite, 'fahr' for fire—has an amazingly positive effect on me."

"It . . . does?" Blair couldn't pull her gaze away. In reality, his eyes were more beautiful than she had remembered. Richer in shading and light, their autumnal depths held a golden gleam of discovery, a glimmer of desire.

"It does," he affirmed with husky conviction, "and I want to hear more, if you'll say yes."

"To . . . what?" The two words passed Blair's lips in a halting whisper. She might have gotten them out in a normal tone if the stroke of his thumb hadn't slowed to a lengthy, repeated circular movement that made her tremble with desire rather than dread.

"To stretching your schedule for a date," he replied, "with me."

Confronted with the most unwelcome request she could imagine from him, Blair gulped and scrambled for a sensible reply. "Oh, I'd just . . . that'd be just . . . but I'll be so busy I just won't have one minute to spare and—"

He put a silencing finger to her lips and tipped her chin up, gazing deep into her eyes. "No one's *that* busy, sugar magnolia. Not even a Type A."

4

POWERS TOOK IN BLAIR'S profoundly amazed and con-
fused expression. *Sugar magnolia.* He felt an urge to re-
move her glasses and murmur those two words a second
time against the soft, pink O of her mouth. The closer he
looked, the better she looked. She was sweet and fra-
grant. *Sugar magnolia.* She hadn't agreed to a date with
him yet.

"Tomorrow?" he prompted. "Dinner?"

"Dinner?" Blair repeated in a breathy whisper. "Tomorrow, I . . . uh . . ."

Powers felt an even stronger urge than before as the tip
of her tongue darted out to wet her lips. He restrained
himself but couldn't resist an exploratory stroke of his
thumb over her moist lower lip to test just how soft and
sweet she would be to kiss.

He hadn't expected that her mouth would tremble at
his touch or that her eyelids would flutter closed for an
instant and fracture his restraint. They did. The break
was fast and clean. His mouth descended to within a
whisper of hers before a short, abrupt upsurge of the elevator snapped his head back.

"Oh!" Blair exclaimed. A down surge of the same distance followed, and their foreheads bumped.

Silently berating the hotel engineer's poor timing, Powers hugged Blair to his side and tucked her head under his chin, bracing her and himself as the cubicle jolted them again, plummeted, then shot higher than the first time, plunged lower than the last.

Burrowing her face into his chest and clutching his shirt for support, Blair felt all shook up inside. She couldn't deny that it was due less to the elevator's fearsome fits and starts than to the fact that Powers had almost kissed her and she had almost allowed it.

Never in her worst-case imaginings had she envisioned such a thing happening. Nor had she ever pictured herself taking shelter from seemingly imminent disaster in Powers Knight's arms, loving every moment of it as well as fearing what might happen if it continued.

Blair burrowed closer into his shoulder and found it as muscular and solid as it had been five years ago. Oh, the sooner she got free of him, the better. Away from him she'd be able to think of more than just the night they had shared. Away from him she'd be able to breathe. Away from him she could put past and present back in focus and stop confusing the two.

Down, up, down the car lurched.

"We'll make it," Powers soothed, tightening his embrace. "Hold on."

Blair held on tighter. At the same instant, the elevator rose up smoothly, up and away.

"There," Powers murmured, dipping his mouth to her ear. "Was I right or was I right?"

"Right," Blair dizzily affirmed, certain of little else.

The warmth of his breath at her ear made her stomach feel bottomless, her head topless. In between, like an air-show stunt plane, her heart was doing loop-the-loops. Which direction was the elevator headed? Not able to say down or up with any certainty, she pulled back from Powers to regain her balance.

"Tomorrow night?" he pressed again. "Are we on?"

"I . . . er . . ."

The elevator hummed to a halt. The doors opened. Blair looked up and saw Matthew looking in and down, his eyebrows raised. A stocky man wearing a brown workman's uniform was standing beside Matthew holding a walkie-talkie to his ear.

"Ah," Matthew smiled. "There you two are. Wisely sitting out the holdup I see."

Abruptly aware that he and the workman *could* see her and Powers, Blair jerked out of his embrace and hurriedly pushed herself upright to a wavery, rubber-kneed stance.

"Steady, there," Powers said, rising beside her and supporting her with the flat of his palm in the small of her back.

The workman, whose hotel name tag identified him as the assistant engineer, stepped into the elevator with them and put the car on temporary hold. He grinned at Powers and said into the receiver, "Guess which VIP you just treated to a joyride, boss?"

"Who?" a gravelly voice inquired.

The assistant engineer grinned. "The general manager."

The voice chuckled. "Better the GM than a guest, Earl. Put him on."

Powers took the handset and said into it, "The GM wasn't the only passenger, Conroy. You and I have some serious apologies to make to the lady I'm with for the shake-up she just experienced."

"Can we make it up to her with dinner on us?"

"Dinner on us," Powers repeated with a tiny smile. "Great idea. Tomorrow night? Upstairs? Eight o'clock?"

"I'll be there, red face, necktie and all," Conroy promised.

"Me, too. And in the meantime, Con," Powers added, "do an in-depth diagnostic on this car and send me a report."

"Roger. Over and out."

Powers handed the phone back to Earl, then bent to retrieve his jacket and Blair's briefcase. Taking Blair's elbow, he led her out of the cubicle to Matthew, who cupped her other elbow with a reassuring squeeze. Behind them the doors closed on Earl's farewell salute.

"A good thing you two had each other for company in there," Matthew said as they walked down the elegantly mirrored hall.

"You can say that again, Pop," Powers agreed.

"A good thing too, son, that you and Conroy are making amends to Blair tomorrow night."

"About dinner," Blair began, "I'm not sure I—"

"He'll be hurt if we cancel," Powers cut in. "Con takes his job and his responsibility to the St. Martin's guests very seriously. When he said his face would be red, he meant it. It's a personal embarrassment to him that the elevator inconvenienced you during your stay here."

Mindful that further involvement with Powers would be complicated, Blair couldn't overlook the golden opportunity of having dinner with Conroy. A hotel engineer so personally devoted to the flawless working of the house machinery would be invaluable to her appraisal of the St. Martin. A mealtime chat with him could be very informative.

"Very well," she said reluctantly, reasoning that a threesome at dinner would be far more manageable than a date with Powers. "I'll see to shufflin' my schedule."

Powers noted that she had agreed, but not to a date. Her flustered reluctance before she'd accepted and her nervous nibbling of her lower lip made him wonder briefly if she found something lacking in him.

He knew that only the rare man who looked closely would see beyond Blair's apparent plainness to her subtle attractiveness. He concluded that her reluctance probably stemmed more from inexperience with men and dating than from any lack on his part.

He still couldn't quite believe he'd asked one of his guests to dinner and almost kissed her in the elevator. It had long been against his personal policy to date hotel guests, and he had never succumbed to temptation. It surprised him that in mere minutes, the sizzle of chemistry between himself and Blair Sansome had overturned years of adherence to his policy.

Unlocking the door to Blair's suite, he cautioned himself that she might well be as virginal as she was obviously inexperienced at the dating game. Type-A directness and speed wouldn't be the proper course. The proper course would be...well, a knightly, measured one that would keep sugar magnolia from wilting with anxiety before he could court her into glorious bloom.

Court? The word caught him off guard. On its heels came a sudden, romantic impulse to sweep her up in his arms and carry her over the threshold into the suite. He flashed a startled glance over her head at his father and caught Matthew looking at him.

Matthew winked like a wise owl. Powers got the itchy feeling that his father had just read his mind.

Don't hold that thought, Pop. Powers conceded to himself that he might carry Blair over a threshold if the chemistry held, but his father could stop mentally brushing off his tux for a wedding.

"Nice suite," Matthew commented, glancing around at the elegant parlor. "Very much like mine. Would you look at that Golden Gate," he marveled at the view from the windows. "And if you have a trick TV like I do, Blair, you have a treat in store."

Blair raised her eyebrows. "Trick TV?"

Powers nodded. "They're standard in every suite."

"You show her how it works, son," Matthew said, walking to the door. "I have some serious unpacking to do." He shut the door behind him.

"Never seen a trick TV?" Powers inquired.

Blair shook her head, wishing the suite had a trick door instead, one through which she could escape Powers and the warmth of his palm on her elbow.

"This way," he directed, steering her into the bedroom. "Here it is." He led her to a big-screen television on a low mahogany chest. It faced an enormous bed. "Now you see it, right?"

She looked from the TV to Powers and back. "Right."

"And now you don't," he said, pressing a corner of the chest. The TV lowered flush into the chest. A second press resurrected it.

"It does the same disappearing act from the remote control, as well," he advised huskily, "and it delivers full cable along with stereo sound."

Blair tried, but she couldn't keep her eyes from meeting his, tried but couldn't pull her elbow from his grasp, tried but couldn't make her feet step back and away from him.

"And," he added, "you're expected in my suite in exactly one hour for cocktails." He slid his palm down her forearm and caught her fingers in his. Holding her helpless gaze, he pressed his lips for a brief instant to the back of her hand, then turned on his heel and left.

An hour. Cocktails. Blair stared at her hand. It was all she could do not to press that pulsing spot to her lips and savor his lingering kiss. *Oh, please,* she thought. She felt behind her for the edge of the bed and sat down hard.

POWERS STOOD IN THE HALL for a long moment and stared at the door he had just closed. Then he headed slowly, unsteadily to his own door. It was so strange. Touching a kiss to Blair's hand had left him with the heart-expanding sensation that he had not only kissed her hand in the past, but every square inch of her body. Which was impossible.

He flexed his hand. The feel of Blair's fingers, the scent and texture of her touch, lingered. He breathed deeply. Until a moment ago, only Love LaFramboise's touch had ever affected him like that.

What had just happened was unprecedented. It meant something. More than something. It meant a lot. He paused in mid-step, struck by a giddy wave of wonder and emotion. Had he found a second Love in Blair?

BLAIR ROSE TO ADMIRE the spectacular view and then got down to business. She double-locked her door, shed her wig and bulky suit, and concentrated on replacing every thought of Powers Knight with thoughts of the job she had come to do at the St. Martin. She reminded herself that she was a persnickety, professional snoop, and snoop she would to the best of her ability.

First on her agenda was a thorough check of her suite. She methodically moved through the parlor, bedroom and bathroom, checking for any evidence of poor maintenance and sloppy housekeeping. She noted each plus and minus on a checklist that was several pages long.

She scrutinized the ceiling for stray cobwebs or water stains, then examined the thick blush-pink carpet for wear, tear and spots. No visible cobwebs, and the carpet looked fresh and clean. She noted vacuum cleaner tracks on the nap. Very good.

Next she finger-wiped every reachable surface for dust. All surfaces proved clean, but a check under the cut-crystal ashtray on the glass coffee table turned up a not-so-faint water ring. On the other hand, the parlor's console TV screen was squeaky clean.

She pushed the On button. A blast of sound blared out from a rock video station. Grimacing, she turned the sound down. A minus. The sound wasn't set low as it should have been. The maid had overlooked a small, but important point. The bellman who had delivered Blair's bags should have checked it, too. It was an oversight one might excuse in an economy hotel, but not in a luxury hotel of the St. Martin's caliber.

Blair examined the electrical cords and plugs in the room for loose connections and exposed wires. More often than not, she mused, it came down to the little things making the big difference. Thinking of little things brought Angel Clare to mind. She smiled as she tested the drapery pull-cords for ease and smoothness of operation.

Ange. She missed him. It had been love at first sight for both of them in the pet shop a year ago. She had dropped in to buy a green turtle for her godson's fourth birthday. Lovestruck, she had bought Angel Clare and a cage and all the necessary birdseed mix and cuttlebone. Only after hurrying home and setting Angel to rights had she remembered about the turtle. She'd had to return to the store.

Recently she had realized that Angel had matured enough to begin needing a mate. That led to thoughts of how much she, herself, craved a mate. That led to thoughts of Powers.

It was painfully clear that Angel Clare wasn't alone in his restlessness for a mate. Blair had procrastinated in searching out a ladylove for him, mostly because she suspected that their billing and cooing would serve as reminders of her nonexistent love life. It was simpler to be single with another single.

Powers is single.

She tapped her finger absently against the phone. Why hadn't he married yet? But she might well ask the same thing of herself. It just hadn't happened, that's all. Still, men as good-looking and exciting as Powers rarely remained single for long except by choice.

But what order of man wakes to find a strange woman joining him under his covers and makes love with her, without any inhibition, after only a moment's pause?

Blair frowned. What order of man, indeed? Free spirits. Sex addicts. Was there a difference? What order of man was he now? Why should it matter what he was then or now?

Blair knew why. It mattered. She had recovered from Jason, but she hadn't felt this intense attraction to any other man since the night she had spent with Powers Knight.

Blair reminded herself that she had no right to judge him. People changed. They grew up, straightened out, took on demanding careers, put their values and priorities in order and put reckless habits behind them.

Yes, people changed, herself included. Her recovery from the breakup with Jason had been surprisingly quick. She had dated for a couple of years and later moved in with a divorced Seattle restaurateur for six months. She and Jeff had parted on neutral terms without any great love lost.

So here she was, single, great job, great condo, great life—and restless for something more.

BLAIR WAS LATE. Powers checked his watch, adjusted his tie and smoothed the lapels of his suit. Though he ran overtime most days, he had little patience with that bad habit in anyone else. Where was she?

Seated in a leather armchair, Matthew lounged back with his feet on an ottoman and his fingers laced behind his head. His eyes were focused on Powers's view of the Golden Gate Bridge and the Marin headlands beyond.

"Just look at that fog creep in."

Distracted, Powers glanced out the window, then at the face of his watch.

"Clock-watcher," Matthew chided. "She'll be along any minute now. Sit back and be patient."

"I can't." Powers stood and jammed his hands into his pants pockets. "I hate to wait."

"You weren't hating to wait when the elevator opened," Matthew observed. "From what I could see, you weren't any too happy to be rescued."

"Maybe I wasn't," Powers muttered.

"I was hoping that might be the case. I knew your mother was the woman for me from the moment I looked closely at her. More closely than any man before me. Like father like son?"

Powers shucked his hands from his pockets and sat down facing Matthew. He propped his elbows on his knees and clasped his hands between them. "Maybe. *How* did you know Mom was the woman for you?"

"Very simple. I couldn't stand the thought of Mary wanting any man but me. It was instantaneous."

Powers thought about Blair wanting a man other than himself. It grated him a little. "Had that happened to you before?"

"No. My experience with women before Mary hadn't been extensive."

Powers focused on his shoes. "Well, it's no secret that mine has been—or at least that it was at one time."

"I do remember when your mother stopped speaking to you in your senior year in college," Matthew said, nodding. "You seemed to have a different coed answering your phone morning, noon and night."

"I was young, then, Pop. That was a long time ago."

They sat in comfortable silence. The past was the past. Powers had never been monklike, but he considered himself a normal healthy male.

His last real indulgence had occurred in response to that irresistible fantasy of fantasies, Love LaFramboise. She had kissed him half-awake from an erotic dream. Dream had mingled with reality in those first intoxicating moments, and he had lacked sufficient strength to resist the combination of male instinct and Love's surprise seduction. Heedless of all else, he had loved the night away with her.

He wondered what Matthew would have done in the same situation, but he wasn't about to ask. That night was a private personal experience he couldn't share with another soul.

So he asked instead, "What do you think of Blair, by the way?"

"Good things. What do *you* think?"

Powers pretended to consider the question gravely. "Me? The Type A who's suddenly a sucker for that slow southern style?"

Matthew chuckled. "My advice is that you adopt a slow style with Blair if you're as interested as I think you are. That should prove a challenge to you, the way you race through life."

"Slow I'll be, Pop. Just what my doctor prescribed."

"For what?"

"The stress coronary he doesn't want me to have."

Matthew sat up and swung his feet off the ottoman. "The what?"

"I knew I shouldn't have mentioned it." Powers glanced beseechingly at the ceiling.

Upset, Matthew stood and repeated, "The what?"

"The heart attack he thinks I'm asking for."

"Heart attack!"

"Now, Pop, calm down."

"Calm down over a stress coronary? How long have you been at risk?"

"It was just a warning." Powers sighed and pushed himself up to face his father. "Look, I've been on the slow-down trail about a week now. I've begun watching what I eat, exercising daily, trying to downsize my workload. I can do it."

Matthew clapped a hand to his son's shoulder, reassured. "You do that, young man. Put your mind to it. Losing Mary before her time to cancer was tragedy enough. Losing you would be . . ."

"I know, Pop," Powers said gently. "I plan to be around a long time."

Matthew turned at a knock on the door. "And there's Miss Louisiana."

"I'm sorry I'm late," Blair apologized when Powers opened the door.

Confronted by him again, she had trouble remembering the excuses she had rehearsed in her rush to get disguised again.

"Late?" Matthew called to her from the wet bar across the room. "Nonsense. You're not at all remiss. What may I get you? A cocktail? Or would wine be preferable?"

"Say a mint julep and you'll make his day," Powers said under his breath as he led her to sit on a blue suede sofa facing a marble fireplace.

"A mint julep would be as fine as fine could be if the fixin's are handy," she said to oblige.

Matthew beamed. "They are, and I'm delighted to tell you the mint comes fresh from the *chef du garni* downstairs in the main kitchen. Powers, what's your poison tonight?"

"The same, please." Powers winked at Blair, then left her for a few moments to lend his father a hand.

Blair looked around appreciatively. Powers's suite was spacious, its furnishings more contemporary in style than the floral decor in hers. Dominant tones of deep blue and pale grey gave it a clear, direct feeling. It was, Blair observed, as frankly masculine as the man himself.

Ultra-conscious of the role she had to play, she commented, "My, my, Powers. Livin' at work makes your commute right short, I'd say."

"That's one of the up sides," he replied.

"The big down side," Matthew interposed, "is living at work, Blair." He spooned sugar into three tall glasses. "This won't be the first time I've said to Powers that a home would suit him better."

"And it won't be the first time I've said to Pop, 'What would I do with a home?'"

"To which *I* answer, 'Everything you don't do at work.'"

Powers pulled a droll smile. "Like mowing the lawn and patching the roof and doing without maid and valet and room service."

"Because he'd rather work day and night," Matthew retorted.

Blair saw opportunity at hand and grabbed it. "Day and night is how I'll be workin', too, right up to check-out come Friday," she said quickly. She drew her forefinger horizontally under her chin. "I'm up to here with business, startin' right after that nice mint julep you're so kindly whippin' up for me."

"Don't forget tomorrow night," Powers said, handing her a brimming, mint-sprigged glass. He settled with his own on the sofa next to her and added, "Conroy won't."

"I've jotted it down," she reassured him. In fact, she had jotted down a list of several leading questions to oh-so-innocently ask Conroy the next night. She was determined to work the occasion for all it was worth to Carroll Management and Wesmar Hotels.

Drink in hand, Matthew sat down in the nearest armchair. He raised his glass and grinned. "To mowing the lawn and patching the roof."

Powers raised his. "To the maid, the valet and a short commute."

Blair raised hers. "To workin' day and night and gettin' the job done."

"I see I'm a loner here, vastly outnumbered by two of a kind," said Matthew, regarding them with feigned disgruntlement. He took a sip of his julep and set it down on the travertine coffee table. "Blair, what company do you work for where toiling at all hours is the order of its day?"

Blair opened her mouth to reply, but Powers beat her to it. "Blair is a CPA. Litigation support is her specialty. Highly technical."

"Highly," Blair chimed in, "and a crashin' bore, except to litigation supporters." The less said on the subject of her sham profession, the better. Any little thing might trip her up.

"Speaking of crashing," Matthew said, "I seem to have acquired a headache. Two aspirin and a catnap should put it to rights, if you'll excuse me." He stood. "Don't get up, son. Ring me for dinner when it's time. Good night, Blair."

Blair couldn't answer. She had gulped her julep when Matthew stood and was trying not to choke. All she could do was nod helplessly. Matthew was out the door before she swallowed, and she was alone, again, with Powers.

"With a cranky elevator and now Pop's headache, I seem to be lucking-out today," he said, stretching his arm out behind her on the back of the sofa and edging a little closer.

Blair edged away. She slid forward and set her drink on the table. "I should be goin', too."

"You'd leave me to drink alone?" Powers inquired, pursing his lips in silent reproach. "All alone, sugar magnolia?"

She sat back warily without reclaiming her glass. "I do have a right tight schedule to keep from runnin' off track."

"So do I, but taking time out for a mint julep won't derail mine more than just a little." He inched closer. "What did you say you were doing for dinner tonight?"

"Meetin' a client."

He nodded and just kept nodding as he looked at her. "I do a lot of working dinners, too," he finally said after studying her just long enough to make her want to squirm. "My doctor says it's bad business, but I'd rather talk business over a meal than eat alone."

"I expect there's a lady or three or four close by who'd sit across from you if you asked real polite-like," Blair couldn't resist pointing out.

He sighed teasingly. "Blair, I asked *you* 'real polite-like' in the elevator, and what did it take to make you say yes?"

"Well, I wasn't quite—"

"Conroy is what it took." His tone softened. "Why? Give it to me straight. Am I barking up the wrong magnolia tree here?"

"Uh . . . yes."

He sat very still. "You wouldn't go out with me even if you had the time?"

Blair flinched. His questions were so honest, her answers so dishonest. She hated to lie. That "yes" had been forced out. The truth was that, under normal circumstances, she would have *made* time to see more of Powers Knight. These circumstances were anything but normal.

"Powers, I'm just not . . ." Oh, where were the right words?

"Not what? Not interested?"

She shook her head, the coward's way out, and tried to do it with conviction.

"You know what?" he said softly.

"What?"

"You're a bad liar, sugar. That's not my ego talking, either. It's the look in your eyes, the blush on your cheeks." He pushed her gravity-prone glasses up from where they'd slipped down. "They tell me you're shy, not used to being rushed by a guy."

The latter was half true, Blair silently conceded as she held her breath under his close scrutiny. She'd had her share of being rushed, but hadn't made time for men after living with Jeff. None had interested her. And Powers, the one man who did, wouldn't want her if he knew who she really was.

"Look, I've never won gold medals for patience, but what if I guarantee I won't rush you?" He cupped her shoulders in his palms and turned her to him. "Will you see me after tomorrow night? An hour here, an hour there, whatever you can spare?"

"I would, but . . ." She could barely breathe.

A corner of his mouth tipped up. "There you go with the buts again. But what, Blair?"

He was so close, so ardent, so persuasive, so energetic. Two words were all she could muster against the onslaught. "Why me?"

His initial reply was a puzzled smile. "Why *not?*" he murmured. "Since we met in the airport, every word you've spoken makes me want to hear more. I've known women who'd love to have skin like yours. They'd want to trade legs with you."

"They'd best have their eyes examined," Blair weakly protested, thinking that *his* eyes could move a woman to do rash and risky things. Everything else about him had the same effect, including his direct approach, his quirky-tender smile, the endearing way he had indulged his father with the juleps, the warmth of his palms on her shoulders, the spice of his after-shave.

"I don't need my eyes examined," he countered. "I see more than you think."

His fingers traced down her cheek to her chin. "Powers," she attempted after a small gulp, "you're terribly nice and all, but I have that client comin' real soon."

"You have something else 'comin' before that, unless you object."

"What?"

"A kiss."

He drew her so near as he said it that Blair could only look at him cross-eyed and wonder at her inability to draw back out of kissing range.

"Any objections?" he whispered an inch from her lips.

She had a multitude of them, somewhere, but the chorus of her senses was overpowering each one. The scent of mint julep and spicy after-shave was a heady intoxicant. The warmth of his whisper coaxed her lips to part, her eyes to close.

Her fingers found their way to his suit lapels and held on tight. His fingers fanned out under her chin. Her mouth rose to his. His mouth lowered to hers.

It started out nothing like their first kiss in the dark of that long-ago night. It began soft and sweet, minty-fresh and ingenuous, all innocent surprise. Then mutually recognized passion moved in all of a sudden and took hold.

A low helpless moan sounded in Blair's throat. Powers echoed it, opening his mouth, urging her to do the same. His tongue touched hers, stroked it. Taste. Oh, he tasted the same as before, Blair thought, only the hint of mint and bourbon making any difference at all. He still kissed like no one else Blair had ever known.

He moaned again, then broke the kiss so abruptly that her head spun. His pupils huge and dark with desire, he stared down at her.

"Blair . . ." His breath shook.

She stared up at him. "Powers . . ." Her breath shook worse than his. "I . . ." She pushed him away, shaken by the passionate response she hadn't been able to restrain. "I have to get goin' right now."

She stood. He looked as dazed and stricken as she felt. Stricken by what? She didn't want to know. She took a wobbly step away.

He reached out and caught her wrist. "Don't. Not yet. Let me apologize. Let me—"

"I'm runnin' late." She threw off his hand, whirled away from him and headed for the door.

He caught up with her just as she reached the door. "Give me just one second, Blair." He covered her hand on the doorknob with his. "Just a kiss was all I had in mind. I never meant more than that." He raked his hand through his hair. "It got away from me." He gave her a confounded, searching look. "You kiss so much like . . ." His voice trailed away.

"No harm done. Thank you kindly for the julep," Blair babbled nervously. She opened the door and hurried into the hallway.

Powers stopped in the doorway. "I won't lose my cool again," he called after her. "Really."

Blair waved a hand without turning around. "Don't worry your head 'bout it," she called back.

Powers watched her flee. It was all he could do not to dog her fast-moving heels into her suite and kiss her again. Minus the cognac he remembered from five years ago, plus the mint and bourbon from tonight, Blair Sansome tasted like Love LaFramboise. Eyes closed, he could have sworn he'd kissed Love in the flesh.

Blair rounded the hall corner at a fast walk. Out of Powers's sight at last, she sprinted the rest of the way to her suite. Inside, she double-locked the door before leaning against it to catch her breath. She pounded her fist soundlessly upon the doorjamb in frustration.

If Lillian could see her now, she thought with a groan, she'd pop every stitch of her appendectomy.

5

BLAIR KNEW THAT the safest thing she could do that night was to wimp out. Unfortunately, the safest thing wasn't what she had been hired to do.

"I'm not a wimp," she said out loud as she changed from her brown suit into an equally dowdy pea-green one.

She couldn't let one kiss, earthshaking though it had been, rule the day. Now that she had semirecovered from it, she was resolved to forge ahead as the capable professional that she was.

"I will not order from room service for dinner tonight and cower here in my room," she continued. "I *will* do the job I came to do. I *will* eat in the coffee shop tonight. I *will* have a drink afterward in the mezzanine cocktail lounge."

In her work it was a given that room service was best tested during the breakfast crunch, rather than at the dinner hour. In the morning, guests wanted their coffee hot and their orange juice fresh, and they wanted both right away. Guests with the time for a leisurely breakfast were rare. Those with a tolerance for cold eggs and bacon after a thirty-minute wait were rarer still.

"If Powers is upstairs in the penthouse dining room with his father right now," she reminded herself, "he can't catch you downstairs doing your thing."

For the first time that day she felt thankful for something. That Matthew and Powers had discussed dinner plans during the limo ride was a godsend. She would complete her initial evaluation of the coffee shop and the lounge before their main course was served. Following her long stretch of bad timing and worse luck, it felt good to offer up a prayer of thanks.

Blair gave herself a final check front-to-back and wig-to-toe in the bathroom mirror. Pea-green was not her color, she observed with a satisfied smile. She had bought the drab suit for a pittance in a Seattle thrift shop, along with the blouse with the prim Peter Pan collar and the circle pin stuck in her lapel.

The shop clerk had commented with a sassy wink, "Fraternity boys called those virgin pins in my day." Blair vowed to wear it night and day for luck.

Blair wondered what it was about her that now attracted Powers. Men like him didn't go around kissing blah brown at the drop of a mint julep, unless he was still as indiscriminate about women as he'd been that night when he hadn't known her from Eve. She didn't know if she should believe the worst of him.

She opened a tube of lipstick and made what looked like an accidental streak on the mirror. She added a streak of soap and splattered water at it, to see if the turndown maid would clean the mirror. Likewise, she applied a dot of nail polish to the countertop.

Turning to the commode, she rolled the toilet paper out long enough to touch the floor. If the maid was up to snuff, it would be re-rolled with the end sheet folded into a trim point when Blair returned.

In the parlor on her way out, she "carelessly" left a tattered one-dollar bill and some loose change on the coffee table. She partially covered them with a book to test both the turn-down maid and the day maid for sticky fingers. A routine hotel guest might not notice the disappearance of a dime or a quarter or even an aged dollar bill, but Blair would record it. It never failed to amaze her how even one penny could tempt a twitchy finger in a hotel room.

Just as amazing was the flip side of employee theft. Hotels suffered enormous losses due to the magnetic fingers of hotel guests. Ashtrays, towels, bathmats, sheets, china, silver—and worse—traveled out of hotels and motels daily in suitcases and carryalls. Blair had heard of entire rooms being stripped of everything totable by registered guests.

She shook her head. Honesty could be hard to come by on both sides. But her concern at the moment was the St. Martin's employees rather than its guests. Blair hoped to find that honesty was the policy for the Wesmar hotel staff. The dollar and seventy-eight cents would remain where it was for the duration of her stay, a constant temptation.

With the suite sufficiently booby-trapped, Blair left for the coffee shop. On the way down in the crowded elevator, she tried not to think of how it had felt to be stranded with Powers. Tried not to think of how he had stroked her hand and sheltered her in his strong embrace. Tried not to think of his warm smile and male magnetism and the way he kissed.

Every thought of Powers seemed to rouse a longing in her. Longing for what? For a night of ecstasy like the one before? Yes. And no.

Yes, it had been the best night of her life. Yes, she had come into her own as a sensual, sexual woman. And no, a night like that couldn't happen again. Her love for Jason had been immature. Even so, hope and love had fueled her desire. Love, hope and Powers—in that order—had made that night incredible.

Blair couldn't very well call this inner longing much more than lust. She wasn't in love—or hoping for it. She stepped off the elevator on the lobby level and crossed to the restaurant. She passed a uniformed bellman, and without slowing her brisk pace, she lifted a credit-card-sized recorder halfway out of the breast pocket of her jacket and spoke into it. "Monday, 7:00 p.m., main lobby. Bellman with no name tag."

She lowered the recorder back into her pocket, feeling like a covert female James Bond on assignment. The thought amused her. She found it exciting being an undercover guest.

In the coffee shop, the hostess greeted her with a friendly smile and willingly seated her in the obscure corner she requested. Blair checked the table setting. Nothing was missing. She decided to order big tonight to taste-test a range of menu items and get a good sense of the restaurant's overall food quality.

She would also pretend to be a finicky eater to try the waiter's patience and professionalism. Blair knew that management expected its staff to sell food and drink as well as serve it, so she would rate his salesmanship.

Blair read the waiter's name tag when he greeted her. "I'll have the barbecued back ribs, Gerry."

"No cocktail or appetizer?"

"No, thank you." Point for Gerry. "Just the ribs—with the sauce on the side." She let him write that down before changing her mind. "Or maybe the salmon mousse. Hmmm, let me see..." She changed her mind three times before settling on the ribs. He scored another point by suggesting a salad before the main course. She chose Caesar.

"Can you make the dressing without anchovy and serve it on the side?" Picky, picky, picky. "I'd also like iced tea, please. No ice. And I believe I'll take the mousse, after all."

"Instead of the ribs?"

"No, in *addition* to them." Gerry's smile was still intact, if a little fixed.

"Anything else, ma'am?"

"Just lemon with my tea. Sliced, not wedged."

Looking only slightly glazed, he left her. Within two minutes he returned with cold un-iced tea and sliced lemon. Blair smiled, watching him leave. Quick, polite, detail-minded restaurant staff was hard to find and keep in force. The St. Martin had a gem in Gerry.

Blair sipped her tea and took in her surroundings. The background music caught her ear. "Too loud and fast for a dining area," she recorded.

Her Caesar salad came exactly as ordered. Blair didn't waste a bite. It was too good, even without the anchovies.

She thought of all the food she'd had to smuggle out of hotels in handbags and briefcases. Whenever possible, she gave untouched portions to the homeless on the streets. Otherwise, she had to dispose of the excess food as best she could. It took ingenuity for evaluators to order several meals a day on the job and not blimp out by eating them all.

She smiled, remembering Lillian's favorite job-story, known as The Case of the Surreptitious Steak. Lillian had ordered a room service dinner at a motel inn, then ordered a steak dinner in the restaurant. She had stuffed the steak and the rest of the meal in her plastic-lined purse. To her puzzlement, the waiter had discreetly searched over, under and around the table before removing the empty dinner plate. His face had been incredulous.

Later, when Lillian had emptied her purse, she saw the object of his search and realized why he'd looked so confounded. Poor man. He'd assumed that she'd eaten her steak, T-bone and all.

Blair had to stifle a chuckle when Gerry served the ribs and the mousse. After he left, she taste-tested the mousse before unobtrusively transferring it to a sealed plastic bag in her roomy purse. She slathered the ribs with the side of spicy sauce and continued her meal, trying to imagine what gourmet fare Powers was enjoying upstairs with his father.

POWERS WAS STARING at Blair through the small, diamond-shaped safety window in the door between the kitchen and dining area. He had slipped downstairs between the first and second dinner courses for a spot check on how the rookie coffee shop manager was doing on her first night at the helm.

Why was Blair alone? Or was her dinner appointment late? The place setting across from hers had been removed, so Blair had to be alone and not expecting company. Had her appointment canceled altogether? If so . . .

Powers rubbed his chin. If so, she was a single woman free for the evening, all alone with nothing to do in a city synonymous with romance. From what he could see of the glop-green suit she was wearing, Cupid wouldn't be seeking her out tonight. Still, the lovely line of her shoulders wasn't completely hidden by the bulky fabric. Blair glanced to one side, and he caught the delicate shape of her profile again, the charming tilt of her nose, the rounded silhouette of her lips.

He thought of how perfect her skin had been to his touch, thought of the sweet fire he had felt and tasted in her kiss. She was hot. A single kiss had proven what he'd suspected. Behind her thick glasses, below her prim collars, beneath her drab suits, Blair Sansome was unvented steam.

After kissing her, he felt less certain of her sexual in-experience. Maybe Blair *was* untried and had gone no further than French-kissing to perfection. With whom had she perfected the art? The fiancé she had mentioned earlier? Damn the man, whoever he was.

That jealous thought took Powers off guard. He had never resented other men—except Jason with Love. The more he saw of Blair, however, the less he'd been think-ing of Love.

He touched his lips with his tongue. *Sugar magnolia.* He looked at her sitting there all alone—sweet and sub-tle and steaming inside—and with no warning some-thing slammed into him.

Pure and simple, it was a primitive desire to possess. Powers had never been a possessive guy, never had to be. Still, he felt as if he'd been punched in the stomach.

Well. Here was a first, he thought. An instant of blind fury at the thought of anyone else laying hands on Blair Sansome? Yep. That's what he'd felt, damned if he hadn't. Or *was* it a first? Hadn't he felt the same thing for Love the morning he had woken up with her? Yeah. And Jason had been in the picture.

That was then. This was right now. Nothing barred the way to this woman. Powers took a step through the door. Except that Matthew was waiting upstairs for him. Powers stepped back into the kitchen. He'd been gone only a few minutes, but a few more would be too many. This was, after all, his father's first night in town.

Powers headed for the elevator. What he couldn't do at this moment, he vowed to do later. After dinner with his father, he would seek Blair out, touch her again, kiss her again, start staking a claim.

Something felt right about her, something he couldn't identify. He hadn't thought a slam to the gut would happen to him a second time. Now that it had, he wasn't stopping cold.

Sugar magnolia. All the way up he felt a little punch-drunk. A second chance. What a break! What luck! What a woman!

Wow, did he love that drawl of hers, the soft light in her eyes whenever she looked into his, her spectacular legs. A man whose career meant more than a lot to him, Powers respected Blair's dedication to her profession.

Matthew greeted Powers with a raised eyebrow and a wise, discerning smile. "Don't *you* look fit to crow," Matthew said. "Either you won the state lottery in your momentary absence, or you ran into Blair. Which?"

Powers was instantly wary. "I ran into her . . . sort of."

"And?"

"I saw her from a distance. That's all."

Matthew nodded. "It was evidently enough."

"Not for what *I* can see you're thinking, Pop."

"Thinking isn't necessary when *I* see it all written on your face," Matthew retorted.

"What?"

"Whatever happened to me with Mary. Quite something when it happens, isn't it? Similar to an enormous blow to the solar plexus, yet totally different at the same time."

"My solar plexus has known Blair for one day."

"One look was all it took me with your mother. If you're as smitten as you look, I'd better start pressing my tuxedo."

"Pop, I'm not racing down the aisle."

"Why not? You've done everything else in your life at top speed."

"Well, *you* haven't—except for the conclusion you're jumping to right now. Put the brakes on, will you?"

Matthew's brown eyes danced with impish glee. "Your grandmother's emerald-cut solitaire would be lovelier than anything you could buy for an engagement ring these days."

"I'm nowhere *near* getting engaged."

"Exactly what happened when you 'only sort of' ran into Blair?"

"I told you. Nothing."

"There's no fooling an old fool, son. How's her business meeting going?"

"She was having dinner all by herself downstairs when I saw her."

"Blair alone? What happened to her appointment?"

"Canceled out, I guess." Powers shrugged, then grinned. "Could you come down with another fake headache after brandy and cigars? If she's got time on her hands tonight, I'm going to be what she does with it."

Matthew beamed. "I feel a twinge already."

DOWN IN THE COFFEE SHOP, Blair was assailed by twinges of her own. They were pangs of regret about how she had first met Powers. Not that she regretted the actual experience. She just wished she had met him for the first time today outside of her job. So much could be different. She could be having dinner with him and Matthew, hoping Powers would kiss her again, hoping she'd be seeing as much as possible of him during her stay.

And after her stay? Yes, then too. And why not? Powers was as attractive, successful, sexy and single as they come. She liked his drive, his air of speed and quick decision. If the past could be wiped out, she could be interested in Powers. She wanted to know even more about him.

She stared, unseeing, at the bones on her plate. Personally and professionally, Powers was proving to be quite a man. Her eyes softened at the memory of him gallantly laying out his coat for her in the elevator. His easy comradeship with Conroy and the desk clerk's respect were evidence of his high standing with the rank and file. It said a lot for his management and personal style. Most appealing of all was the kind, loving, humorous side he had revealed with his father.

"Are you finished, ma'am?"

Blair blinked and looked up at Gerry. "Yes." Time for his final test. "Would you bring my check, please?"

"No coffee or dessert tonight? The pastry chef wins Cordon Bleu ribbons for his blueberry tarts."

A-plus all the way. "No, thank you. Just the check."

When he brought it, she paid cash and left a generous tip. "Gerry," she told her pocket recorder on the way to the cocktail lounge, "is a gem."

Pausing in the doorway, she surveyed the lounge. The decor was casually elegant. One could feel comfortable ordering a beer or a fine champagne here. Blair walked in and slid onto the only empty stool at the bar.

The bar was dark-veined green marble with mahogany trim, her low-backed seat was a soft buff leather. On her right sat a middle-aged couple, on her left a man in a business suit. He glanced at her as she sat down. That glance was enough, for he turned back to his drink and whatever he'd been saying to the woman on his left.

Blair pushed her glasses up, feeling mildly stung by his instant disinterest. Though not accustomed to stopping traffic with her face and figure, she wasn't in the habit of going unnoticed by men. As much as she disliked unwelcome male attention, she wasn't sure she liked being dismissed, either. The bartender seemed just as intent on ignoring her.

After a few seconds of eavesdropping, she knew the man next to her was trying to pick up the woman next to him. She heard the discomfort and stress in the woman's evasive replies. Blair's glance at his target's reflection in the mirror behind the bar confirmed that his attentions were unwelcome. Blair suddenly felt fortunate to look plain enough to go unnoticed.

The inattentive bartender was in his mid-thirties, and he had the look of a second-string college athlete. Three comely young women at his end of the bar appeared to be quite enamored of him. In the midst of a round of laughter, he intercepted Blair's gaze and made a leisurely trip to where she waited.

"What can I pour for you?" he asked when he finally got there.

Blair was irritated at the way he looked just past her as he placed a square napkin in front of her. It was clear that the air space above and beyond her left shoulder held a greater fascination for him than she could personally hope to capture. It was also clear that he had no interest in setting the lone wolf on her left straight about hassling unattached females.

She checked out his name tag. Joe. If Gerry was a gem, Joe was a jerk.

"I'll have a gin and tonic, please."

Without even nodding to acknowledge her order, he sauntered back to the end and mixed three drinks to augment his harem's half-full glasses. Joe rang up none of those drinks on the cash register after serving them. He rang hers up, after taking far too long to mix and serve it. So, she thought, he was a jerk *and* dishonest.

She sipped from her glass and glanced around the rest of the bar. Little escaped her notice. Several ashtrays were almost overflowing with butts due to Joe's active neglect. A bar customer at the opposite end had to signal twice for a refill. The predator on her left was refusing to take no for an answer.

Having been in identical situations herself, Blair was furious with Joe for not intervening as a first-rate bartender in a first-rate bar should have done. It was his duty to exercise firm tact in putting this man straight. Joe showed no sign of even noticing the hassle, much less of expending any of his idle energy on it. Once she filed her evaluation, Joe would get just what he deserved for his inexcusable conduct. Fired.

And the barracuda on her left would get just what he deserved, too, she decided. If Joe wouldn't intervene on behalf of a besieged female bar patron, she would. Blair bumped her full glass of gin and tonic right into the man's lap.

6

THE MAN WAS HORRIFIED. His expression was priceless. He was also speechless.

"Mercy!" Blair exclaimed. "How cotton pickin' clumsy of me. I'm plumb sorry, I am."

"I'm not," the woman said, with a grateful look at Blair. "Thank you so much." She held up an empty martini glass. "I'd have done that myself with a fresh drink."

Sputtering, the man grabbed Blair's napkin, his napkin, the woman's napkin. Ice cubes fell onto the floor as he brushed them from his soaked crotch. Blair made no move to help, just looked helpless and observed his futile efforts to mop up.

The commotion unglued Joe from his harem. True to form, he arrived at the accident scene with no bar towel in hand.

"Men's rest room's out the door and two turns to the right," he advised his waterlogged customer.

After a vicious glare at Blair and the woman, the lone wolf eased his bottom gingerly off of his stool and stood, bent forward at the waist. Like a washed-up jockey suffering a severe case of bowlegs, he shuffled out of the lounge.

He had no idea that his undignified exit was being televised by hidden cameras to a closed-circuit TV screen in the St. Martin's security office. Powers and Dominic Borello, chief of security, were observing the bar action.

"Joe's outta here," Borello said, shaking his head.

Powers nodded. "He's history at the end of his shift tonight."

"That was one classy move by the plain dame with the booze." The portly chief of security shifted in his seat. "Froze Romeo's assets but good."

Powers fixed Borello with a flat stare. "She's not a dame."

"Like I said, the beauty queen with the drink," Borello rescinded after missing a beat out of sheer surprise. He tipped the ash from his cigar into his empty coffee cup. "Sorry. I didn't know you knew her."

Powers relaxed and shrugged. "Forget it, Dom."

"She must have legs if you're on her trail," Borello commented with a knowing grin. They had worked together for a year at Wesmar's Chicago hotel where Borello had granted Powers 'honorary *paisan*' status. Their separate transfers to the St. Martin had teamed them happily as coworkers again.

"Not that it's any business of yours, but you're right. Her legs are to die for," Powers confirmed, "and so is her Southern accent."

"Sounds to me like that ain't all. Come clean, man. What's the whole story?"

"Beats me. She's just different, Dom. Nicer, maybe, than anyone I've met in a while."

The chief drew long and thoughtfully on his Havana. "Nice? Sounds like maybe you've been hit hard."

"Maybe."

"Who is she?"

"A Seattle CPA by way of New Orleans."

"A guest?"

"Don't ask."

Borello squinted through a cloud of smoke. "This is a first, if I get what you're not quite saying."

"You get it. Keep your eyes closed if you catch me breaking a personal rule or two any time in the next few days."

"I'm a blind mute, Powers," Borello assured him.

"Good. Stay that way."

"Hey, it comes natural to me. I'm Sicilian, ain't I? Twice removed, maybe, but still up to the code of silence."

"You're a crude, rude ex-cop and the best security man a hotel could have, I might add."

Borello laughed. "I love you, too, you yuppie WASP. Who else would I work nights for to clinch a case against a crooked barkeep?"

Powers turned to view the monitor again. Blair hadn't struck him as the type to drink in a bar alone. She looked vulnerable and alone to him as the hidden camera slowly panned over her in its constant survey of the bar. Joe hadn't replaced her drink yet. Ice cubes were strewn on the floor, a safety hazard. If she stepped on one and slipped . . .

He felt an urge to rush the bar, sweep Blair up, and carry her away from every hazard she could possibly face. He felt like punching Joe and that guy out for looking right through her. As much as her suit and hairstyle and thick glasses subjected her to male callousness, why was she alone in a hotel bar?

"No offense," Borello said, following Powers's gaze, "but a new haircut would be a plus on her. A new suit wouldn't hurt, either."

Powers's frown deepened. "That's all surface. Underneath she's..." He paused in concentration, then looked at Borello. He said hesitantly, "What do you want to bet she's a hooker and not a CPA at all?"

Borello heaved himself out of his chair for a closer look. After a prolonged scrutiny of the image, he pronounced, "No bets. If she's a hooker, I'm a saint. All I see is a lady who can use a makeover. And if I was as hard hit as you seem to be, I'd get down and invite her out of there. A bar's no place for a lady alone."

"It happens to be one of the finest bars on the West Coast, Dom, except for the bartender."

"To a Sicilian, it's still no place for a lady," Borello retorted. "If she was my lady, I'd have her out of there in two minutes flat."

A minute and forty-five seconds later, Joe snapped to attention. He began hurriedly emptying ashtrays as Powers strode into the cocktail lounge. "Good evening, Mr. Knight," he said unctuously.

"Where is she?" Powers demanded, stopping at the stool Blair had occupied.

"Who?"

Powers growled, "The woman who froze Romeo's assets."

"You mean the one who spilled her—"

"Which way did she go? I'm in a hurry."

Joe paled. "How do you know she spil—"

"Romeo called and complained," Powers lied.

"Wow, that was fast," said Joe, looking relieved. "She asked where the closest ladies' room was. I told her and she headed that way."

"Decent of you, Joe. For your just reward, drop into the food and beverage manager's office after your shift, tonight, would you?"

"Reward?" Joe smugly puffed out his chest.

Powers nodded. "See your manager. Clean up this ice, too, Joe, and wipe down the stool before it stains. Good night." He turned away. "And goodbye," he added under his breath. "You're history at this hotel."

Powers stalked to the ladies' room. Was Blair in there or not? Had he missed her? He paced outside the door, jingling the change in his pockets in frustration. Women passed in and out of the rest room. Five times he stopped to see who was leaving; five times the woman wasn't Blair.

He checked his watch. Why did females take so damned long? The door opened a sixth time. He whipped around. The powder room attendant bustled out, a garrulous retiree who worked part-time.

"Mr. Knight," she said with a big smile. "How-de-do."

"I'm doing fine, Philomena, fine. Where are you off to?"

"My break. I pushed it back thirty minutes, it's been so busy."

"Before you go, Philomena—" Powers drew her aside "—have you noticed a woman in an awful green suit in there?"

Philomena nodded vigorously and blurted, "The one with the virgin pin? She's—" Realizing her blunder, she clapped her hand over her open mouth.

"Inside?" He pointed at the door.

She nodded.

"Thank you." He gave her a full-bore smile. "Love those virgin pins."

"Mr. Knight, you are bad," she teasingly accused, lowering her hand to smile back at him. She sidled away a few steps and then fled the scene, giggling like a schoolgirl.

Powers jingled his change happily now, in anticipation. He rehearsed what he'd say to Blair when she came out.

Blair was counting herself lucky that Philomena had stepped out. It was easier to inspect the area without her there. Other than noting a stall door with a dysfunctional lock, however, she could find nothing else of a negative nature to report.

"Philomena runs a tidy operation here," she said into her recorder. She freshened her lipstick. Next, she decided, she would test the concierge. She felt fairly safe she wouldn't run into Powers. He undoubtedly had a lot to catch up on with his father. She pushed the restroom door open.

"Oh! P-Powers."

"Hi," he said, steadying her with his hands at her shoulders and forgetting every polished phrase he'd rehearsed. "I hear you've got some unexpected time on your hands."

"Time?" she squeaked. Her heart was racing. "Me?"

"Who else? I saw you in the coffee shop alone earlier," he explained, "and just a while ago in the lounge."

Blair couldn't absorb the incomprehensible. He'd seen her? How? From where? She stared up at him, dazed.

"What happened, Blair? Cancellation?"

Unable to string coherent answers together as fast as he was asking questions, she could only nod in response. Feel in response. Oh, the warmth of his hands where he held her shoulders. He was so tall, so alive with energy and dash. She felt rattled, dazzled, extra-sensitized, overpowered. He was too much.

"How about a walk around Union Square?" he urged. "Pop's racked out again with that headache. Must be the altitude or something." Powers knew he was babbling like an idiot. Somehow it didn't matter. He was saying what he really wanted to say. That he wanted to be with her. Now.

"A walk," she repeated, surprised that her mouth could still form whole words. She tried for an actual sentence. "That sounds . . ." Terrific or terrifying? Both.

" . . . Like the best idea you've heard all day," he prompted, taking her elbow and escorting her down the curved, carpeted stairs from the mezzanine to the lobby.

Knowing she shouldn't be doing it, yet doing it anyway, Blair walked out through the main door with him.

The fresh air was bracing, just what she needed. He tucked her hand in the crook of his elbow and hugged it close to his side.

"Warm night," he commented. "No fog. Moon's almost full. Nice, huh?"

"Nice as nice can be." Blair fell into stride with him.

"Do you get fog in Seattle, Blair? I don't remember any that one time I was there."

"Oh, yes. We get a wisp here and there. A passel of rain here and there, too."

Powers squeezed her hand against his side. "How much is a passel, sugar magnolia?"

"Enough to keep Seattle the Emerald City year after year."

"Passel," he repeated, savoring the word by imitating her accent as he said it. "Did I mention that the way you talk does things to me?"

"I b'lieve you did."

"I did? When?"

"In the stuck elevator."

"Oh. That seems like a lifetime ago right now. You were so frightened. And I don't blame you. I'm glad I was there to—" he slowed and slid her hand from his elbow and curved his arm around her shoulders "—do this." Stopping completely, he turned her to him. Tilting her chin up with his forefinger, he added, "And then this." Sweeping his thumb gently over her lower lip, he added again, "And then this." Bending his head, he touched his lips to hers for only an instant. "And finally this."

"You didn't do that," Blair got out in the fleetest of whispers.

"I wanted to, Blair." He moved his arm from her shoulders to her waist and pressed her against him. "I want to now. More than I can tell you without doing it. You tasted so sweet when I finally *did* do it, so good."

Blair wondered how it was possible to feel each button of his suit outlined against her, yet have only a floating sensation in her feet. She had no sense of solid ground, no realistic perception of being in the center of a public square where people sat on the benches or strolled on the crisscrossed sidewalks. There was only Powers and herself. She was drawn to him by forces she couldn't control.

Her fingers sought his suit lapels. She was surrendering and she knew it. She wanted what he wanted.

"Kiss?" he whispered.

"Kiss."

It didn't describe the perfection of their fit. Their lips were made for each other. The meeting of their tongues was sensual, then sexual, then sense-shattering.

Blair felt herself and Powers tremble at the same moment.

Powers moaned, then tore his mouth from hers. "Blair," he said in a strangled whisper, "patience isn't my strong point, but I'm trying. You have to understand that. Do you?"

Dizzy and unsure of whether she understood anything, she managed to whisper back, "Yes...I know..."

Eyes closed, he rested his forehead against hers. "Good." He sighed. "If I get going too fast . . . well, tell me to cool it." He lifted his head and looked down at her. "Okay?"

She slid her hands down to his lapels again, rested her cheek against his chest and nodded. She was promising herself that she wouldn't kiss him or get this close to him again. More of this would mean greater closeness, personal involvement. More of this just couldn't be.

"Cool it," she made herself say. "I have papers to get ready for tomorrow. We should be gettin' back."

His response was a huge, reluctant sigh of assent. "Back we go," he agreed. Keeping one arm around her, he smiled and placed a quick, sweet peck of a kiss on the tip of her nose. Hand-in-hand they retraced their steps.

He was as silent during the stroll back to the hotel as he had been talkative before. A few times along the way he smiled down at her. They stopped to watch a cable car roll by.

"Let's ride one while you're here," he said as they crossed the street in its noisy wake. "Tomorrow night after dinner?"

"We'll see."

He stopped her right there in the middle of the crosswalk at Geary and Powell. "Why 'we'll see' and not 'yes, I'd love it?'" he asked, his eyes candidly searching hers.

"Well, I *would* love it—the cable cars bein' so famous and all—but I'd feel bad cancelin' out if somethin' comes up." She took a step forward. He halted her with a pull on her hand. "Lordy, Powers, we're in the middle of the street," she protested.

"I know," he replied, "and I'm not moving until I get something straight. Do you want to see more of me or not?"

Blair saw the Walk signal switch to Don't Walk. The traffic light was about to change. "We're goin' to plumb get run over standin' here, Powers."

"Do you or don't you? Why am I getting crossed signals all of a sudden?"

"You're gettin' a red light any minute now is what you're gettin'," Blair contended with a glance up at the lights.

"Tell me, Blair." He gripped her hand firmly. "Am I making a fool of myself with you?"

She opened her mouth to say yes. The light turned red. "No!"

Grinning, Powers pushed her ahead of him through the crosswalk in the nick of time. Safe from the onrush of traffic, Blair turned and confronted him on the tourist-crowded street corner.

"What if I had said yes?"

"I'd have stopped traffic and changed your mind."

Peeved at herself for saying the wrong thing, peeved at him for eking it out of her, she made another effort to pull her hand from his and succeeded this time. "You're plumb crazy, doin' a thing like that."

"I wanted to know. Now I know."

Blair turned away in a huff and started walking. For the first time, except for when he had kissed her, she was finding it difficult to stay in character to match her disguise. Only the accent was coming easy for her.

"You know what I said," she retorted over her shoulder. "You don't know what I was thinkin'."

"I know you were thinking yes when you were kissing me," he countered, looking pretty huffy himself.

Peripherally aware of the odd glances passersby were giving her and Powers, Blair flushed at the idea of what *they* must be thinking. She was glad she was in disguise and not her real self. She was mortified to be arguing kisses and yesses with a man on a busy street corner. She couldn't see why Powers wasn't mortified, as well. As the head of the refined, prestigious St. Martin, he should have been considering his public image.

But he didn't look one bit embarrassed. He looked provoked. Worse, he looked ready to pull her up on her tiptoes and prove his point by kissing her again.

"I wasn't thinkin' at all right then," she defended as calmly as she could.

"That makes two of us," he said after a moment, matching his tone to hers. "Let's go back, shall we?"

They walked silently to the St. Martin, without touching, glancing at each other every few steps of the way. They rode up in the elevator with the two other couples who got off on the fourth floor.

The door closed. Powers looked at Blair. She looked back.

"I'm sorry," he said. "I didn't cool it very well."

"I'm sorry, too." She relaxed with a small smile.

He matched it and quipped, "Our first fight."

"Disagreement," she corrected.

"Whatever." He shrugged, then edged close with a glint in his eyes. "Want to kiss and make up?"

She wished she could stare him in the eye and lie. She couldn't. She lowered her gaze to the knot of his striped silk tie. She wanted badly to nod, but she forced her head to move side to side.

"Look at me straight and do that, Blair."

Slowly, she forced her gaze back to his. She couldn't shake her head. Nor, in the moment of truth that followed, could she halt the slide of his fingers down her arm to her hand. He lifted it to his lips and pressed a kiss upon the lowest knuckle of her middle finger.

Blair drew in a catchy breath. It came back out in an even catchier whisper. "Powers . . ."

"I hear you. I'm cooling it." He kissed her knuckle to the right of middle and her knuckle to the left of middle.

"But, Powers . . ."

He lipped the base of her baby finger. "What, sugar?"

"All this kissin' and makin' up is . . ."

"Better than going to bed mad," he filled in, his breath moist against her skin.

Bed? Blair had a sinking feeling accompanied by a sudden, vivid picture of him leading her to bed by the very hand he was kissing. Bed. This had to stop, she helplessly thought. She had to stop it. Or he had to stop it. *Someone* had to stop it.

A moment later, it stopped. The elevator door opened on their floor and they stepped out. Powers stopped kissing Blair's hand, but he didn't let go.

At her door, he squeezed her fingers. "I'll see you tomorrow night if I don't see you before then."

"I'll be busy startin' right off with a breakfast appointment in the mornin'," she hastened to say.

"And *I'll* be looking forward to 7:00 p.m.," he rejoined. "So will Conroy. Now, where's your key?"

She fished it out of her suit pocket and slid it into the lock. After stepping inside, she paused. "Good night, Powers."

"Good night, sugar magnolia." He tortured her middle knuckle with one last kiss and walked away to his suite.

Blair closed her door and double-locked it. She flopped down on the parlor sofa and expelled a huge, loud sigh of relief and frustration. She hadn't known that hands could be orgasmic.

She looked around the room. What was a huge vase of—magnolia blossoms?—doing on the writing desk? Blair snatched off her glasses. Magnolias, no doubt about it. No doubt, either, of who had sent them. Squeezing her eyes shut, she groaned. Nothing could have reminded her more of Powers and all that had gone wrong in one short day. One cotton-pickin', grit-crackin', stomach-stompin', mind-splittin' day.

From where she sprawled, Blair eyed the ivory envelope that was attached to the crystal vase with an ivory satin ribbon. Why read the note? Why make the day any worse than it had already been?

"Masochist," she muttered at herself as she got up from the couch and crossed to the writing table. The lemon scent of the two enormous white blossoms in the vase wafted to her. They were creamy white, their outer petals unfurled, their inner ones tightly budded. Gold-veined, waxy-green magnolia leaves framed the exotic arrangement. "Masochist," Blair muttered again and opened the envelope.

The note inside read:

One from me. One from Pop. He's tickled pink because you asked for a mint julep. Thanks. I'm tickled, too. Because of you.

Yours, Powers.

Blair couldn't put it down. She didn't want to melt over the last eight words in the note, but she did. She didn't want to go limp and helpless, but she did. She didn't want to read them over and over until each word was etched in her memory, but she did so until they were.

She couldn't help herself, for here was romance. More than that, here was *personalized* romance. What woman could be immune to it at the hands of Powers Knight? He could have sent roses. He could have sent carnations or gardenias or orchids. But, no, he hadn't.

Sugar magnolia. Blair had never felt quite so special, so individually appreciated, so singled out by a man as his perfect choice of flowers and written words showed. She wasn't fooled for a minute about Matthew's purported share in it. One hand had drafted the note. One knowing man had known *the* flower to choose. No man in her life had ever done anything so romantic for her.

Before she went to bed, Blair moved the vase and the note to her nightstand, knowing even as she did that they were no help to her cause. She told herself that she wanted the blossoms nearby because they were so lovely, their fragrance so redolent of her childhood in New Orleans.

That was all.

Not because they were from the most exciting, romantic man she had ever met.

Not that at all.

7

THE MAGNOLIAS WERE the first thing Blair saw the next morning when she woke. She closed her eyes. Added reminders of Powers were almost too much after dreaming about waking up in each other's arms five years ago.

Everything had happened in the dream as it had in reality—an accurate, precise, explicit replay of the morning after their night together. Scene by scene. That morning . . .

A SLIGHT COGNAC HANGOVER made her reluctant to open her eyes when his caressing fingers brought her gently out of sleep. Lying on her side, she drowsed lightly as his fingers adored her left breast. A warm, hard chest pressed against her back. Soft breath warmed her shoulder.

"More," she sleepily requested of that adoring hand.

His fingertips responded and traced spirals around her nipple, fanning it to hardness. Then fingertips joined with thumbtip to cup her budded flesh. Drawing out and pressing in, the motion summoned a sleepy sigh of pure pleasure from her.

"More . . . more . . ."

A shift of his legs behind her bent her knees and brought an instantly identifiable rigidity against the curve of her bottom. So hard, again. Aroused, she wriggled her hips invitingly, felt the wet heat of an open kiss on her shoulder blade, the rasp of morning beard, a nip of teeth, a whirl of tongue to soothe the love-bite. Shivers of sensation were bringing her out of sleep. She wanted more. . . .

His hand slid down the curve of her ribs to the slope of her waist and up the rise of her hip. He walked his index and middle fingers to her navel, and around it. She placed her hand over his and led it between her thighs to where she burned for his touch.

His long, talented fingers mastered her with breath-robbing skill. She squirmed and gasped and reached back to stroke him, to prompt him. At last, he slid into her, but his fingers never left her, even when she groaned with delight at being so filled with him, even when his hips bucked against her with growing force and speed.

With his combined touch and bucking thrusts she climaxed with a cry, and only then did he allow himself his own satisfaction. After that, after the long, sated drift down, she turned in his arms and opened her eyes to say what was in her heart.

"Oh, Jason, I love—" Heart. Breath. Speech. Sound. Everything stopped except the power of sight.

It was a calamitous instant of discovery. Astonished, appalled, she looked into a face she had seen only in Jason's college yearbook. His eyes opened languorously and met hers as she stared. A split-second later they mirrored her horrified expression.

"Oh, my God!" They both gasped.

"You're not—not *him!*"

"You're—you're *her!*"

Moving as far apart as they could from each other while remaining covered by the sheet they shared, they regarded each other wide-eyed, tousled and breathless across Jason's double bed.

"I thought you were—" they both began. They groaned together, "You're—oh, my *God!*"

They tried to bolt from the bed in opposite directions. The sheet jerked them back on the mattress, refusing to rip down the middle.

Blair cowered under her half of the sheet, glancing wildly around. One of her black nylons was draped over the lampshade, her lace demi-bra was looped around his ankle. The nylon's mate decorated the headboard. Her frantic glance fell on Jason's nightstand where a framed photo of herself smiled back at her.

"Oh, no!" she cried.

Powers sank back onto a pillow and shook his head in disbelief.

"This isn't happening," he muttered, wiping a hand down his face. "I'm not—it can't be," he continued disjointedly. "I'm asleep...dreaming...one of those crazy ones where you'd swear you're not...but you are...and then you wake up . . . and it's all thin air . . . and . . ."

He stopped short then and stared at her. "We aren't a dream," he said, incredulous, as much to himself as to her. "You . . . you thought I was Jason, didn't you?"

Blair squeezed her eyes shut and nodded. "I know who you are now. From Jason's yearbook."

"And I," he said, shaking his head, "thought you were someone who Jason . . ."

She opened her eyes at his hesitation. "Who Jason what?"

"Never mind. I didn't know you were her." Powers waved a hand at the photo. "His fiancée, I mean." He gave her a sidelong look. "He's not here. Told me he won't be back for a day or so."

She clenched her teeth and clutched as much of the sheet to herself as she could without moving closer to Powers. "Why are *you* here?"

"Semester break at grad school."

"Where is Jason?"

"Out of town somewhere."

"Somewhere?"

"He wasn't clear on where, okay?" Another sidelong glance and he blurted, "All I know is he should have been here. You were out of this world."

Hot tears of humiliation welled up and rolled out onto her cheeks. "Damn you!" she cried. "It wasn't for *you*."

Bent on flight, she yanked the sheet from his grasp and whirled off the bed. His moment of surprise provided her an indelible image of man at his best before his hands shot out to cover his groin. She fled into the living room and threw on her clothes in fevered panic. She was almost dressed when Powers came in shirtless, wearing jeans, and handed her the lingerie and spiked heels she had worn to seduce him. She stuffed them into her purse as fast as she could.

"As true as it was, I'm sorry I said that," he mumbled.

"*I'm* sorry this happened," she replied through her tears.

"Are you that much in love with him?" he asked, watching the garments disappear with hungry eyes.

"Of course I am! We're engaged."

"So where's your ring if you're engaged?" He helped her with her raincoat when she couldn't find the armholes in her rush to escape.

"I took it off."

"Why?"

She whirled on him, purse in hand on the way to the door. "Because last night wasn't about that."

"What was it about?" he asked, following her.

"None of your business."

He stepped in front of her, barring the door. He shoved his hands into his back pockets, looking too male and sexy and blond for words. He said, "I'm in the middle of it now. I want to know."

Blair was almost hysterical with panic and chagrin. "Why? So you can tell Jason that his future wife is a cheap tramp?"

"No, I—"

"No? After everything I said and did? After I proved all night that I can't tell him from you in the dark if I've had one cognac too many?"

"No. I'm not breathing a word. He's a friend I don't want to lose over a mistake like this."

"A fine friend you are to *him*," she observed brokenly, "sleeping in his bed with a woman you've never met. Didn't it occur to you it might be me?"

"No more than it apparently occurred to you that I wasn't him," he retorted. He spoke more gently. "You take the pill, I hope."

"I most certainly do," she tearfully confirmed. "Now let me go."

He stood firm and asked softly, "You never had a clue? Not one?"

"Do I look like I had a clue? How can you ask that?"

"Love, I lockered and showered with Jason on the swim team." He added gently, "Guys compare. He's not me in at least one respect."

Fresh, infuriating tears had sprung to her eyes at his certainty of the truth. "*I* wasn't comparing. How dare you imply that I should have been." With trembling fingers, she dashed the tears away.

"Look, you're in no shape to run out of here like this. Calm down before you go. Blow your nose. Have a bite to eat. A cup of coffee. Something."

"I can't," she told him, sniffing back her tears. "I'm due at work an hour from now."

"Where?"

"At the Four Seasons Hotel. I'm a management trainee." She wiped her eyes. "I have to go."

Stepping aside, he said, "Just for the record, Love, I know good sex. I've never had it as good as with you."

"That's the cheapest parting shot I've ever heard," she flared, jerking the door open.

"I didn't mean it cheap. I hope *you* never had it so good, either."

"And *I* hope never to see you again—especially not at my wedding!"

She walked away from Jason's door, out of Powers Knight's life.

BLAIR OPENED HER EYES. *Never had it so good.* And here she was in Powers Knight's hotel, staring at the magnolias he'd sent her!

The phone rang. She checked the alarm clock. This was her wake-up call, on the dot. The St. Martin was starting the day well.

"Hello?"

"Good morning. It's 7:00 a.m., fifty-two degrees outside, and slightly foggy."

Blair started slightly. It was the voice she'd been dreaming about. She sat up, determined that Powers wouldn't affect her.

"Is it mornin' already?"

"I snitched your wake-up call from the operator. Do you mind?"

"Well, now, a get-up call is the same, never mind who makes it, I guess."

He chuckled. "Listen, Pop and I are having breakfast in the coffee shop in about two minutes. Could you join us for a cup before your appointment?"

"I sure 'nough would love to—and thank you kindly for askin'—but I didn't finish preparin' that presentation last night and—"

He cut in. "Just thought I'd ask on the off chance. Tonight seems a long way off, and I wanted to hear your voice. It does things to me, remember? Good things."

Blair tried to put a dry note in her drawl. "I surely do remember. You're repeatin' it often enough."

"I'm not seeing you often enough. Our walk last night was too short. Did you get the flowers?"

"Why, hush my mouth if they aren't bloomin' beauties to beat all. I thank you, and your daddy, too. Your note was pure charmin'."

"You're welcome. You're sure about that cup of coffee?"

"Sure as seashells on the seashore."

"Sayshells, sayshore. What's to become of my good health when you take the South back to Seattle, sugar? Tell me."

"Um, I've got to get crackin' here on my presentation, Powers. And then I have breakfast with my client."

"In the coffee shop?"

"No. Out."

"Too bad. We could have at least waved across the tables. See you tonight, Blair."

"Bye for now, Powers."

Blair cut the connection and sank back into her pillows. Seeing Powers first thing in the morning would be wonderful. Thinking like that wouldn't do, however. She had to stop dreaming and get back to work.

She dialed room service. The order clerk answered right away, cheerfully. Blair ordered a large breakfast to evaluate cold and hot foods, then got out of bed to take a quick shower. While she was at it, she'd test the availability, pressure and temperature of hot shower water at prime time. Her day had begun.

"TWO WAITERS QUIT yesterday, and we're swamped, but we can handle it, PDK," the St. Martin room service manager informed Powers D. Knight.

"Good show, OTD," he said. "You can have your desk and phone back. I'm through." He got up from Olivia T. Downey's desk where he had just finished his quick call to Blair.

Powers didn't stand on ceremony with his department managers. His executive style was interpersonal rather than aloof. Managers who preferred formality addressed him as Mr. Knight. Others addressed him by his first name.

In their first briefing, Olivia had jokingly pointed out that his sign-off initials could also stand for Pretty Damn Kwick. That said it all for the way Powers operated. Hers could stand for On The Double, Powers pointed out, which said just as much for the way room service went about things. Under Olivia's direction, service at the St. Martin was outstanding.

He walked out to the main order desk with her. As she had indicated, it was swamped with calls. Three clerks wrote out orders as fast as they could take them. Powers scanned a few of the most recent orders.

"Good, good," he approved. "Love it when they order like starving lumberjacks. If we're swamped, at least it's not with nickel-dime stuff." He stopped at one particular sheet and held it up to the clerk. "This just come in?"

The clerk nodded. "One minute ago, sir. Your floor, isn't it?"

"Yeah, my floor," Powers muttered. "You double-checked the suite number and name?"

"Sure did," the clerk confirmed. "She didn't think she wanted strawberry blintzes with everything else, but I sold her on them."

Olivia smugly raised her eyebrows. "Do I have my people trained or do I have them trained?"

"They're trained," he acknowledged, continuing to study the order. Looking up at the clerk again, he asked, "You're sure this is service for one?"

"Yes, sir. I double-checked that, too. One, she said."

"What's the problem?" Olivia inquired, taking the order from Powers. She scrutinized it. "What do you see that I don't besides one very hungry B. Sansome in the Golden Gateway suite?"

"What I see is making me wonder," he replied. "Mind if I tie up your office for one more call?"

Olivia grinned. "Not if you make it PDK. I have two new waiters to interview in there OTD."

BLAIR WAS DISGUISED in her brown suit and wig before room service could reasonably be expected. She switched the radio on while she waited. According to the traffic adviser, a three-car pileup had traffic stopped cold on the Golden Gate Bridge. When the announcer turned to the sports report Blair clicked the radio off. She conducted

PLAY
HARLEQUIN'S

LUCKY HEARTS
GAME

AND YOU COULD GET

★ **FREE BOOKS**
★ **A FREE 20" NECKLACE**
★ **A FREE SURPRISE GIFT**
★ **AND MUCH MORE**

**TURN THE PAGE AND
DEAL YOURSELF IN** →

PLAY "LUCKY HEARTS" AND YOU COULD GET...

★ Exciting Harlequin Temptation® novels—FREE
★ A 20″ Necklace—FREE
★ A surprise mystery gift that will delight you—FREE

THEN CONTINUE YOUR LUCKY STREAK WITH A SWEETHEART OF A DEAL

When you return the postcard on the opposite page, we'll send you the books and gifts you qualify for, absolutely free! Then you'll get 4 new Harlequin Temptation® novels every month, delivered right to your door months before they're available in stores. If you decide to keep them, you'll pay only $2.69* per book—that's a saving of 30¢ off the cover price plus only 49 cents postage and handling for the entire shipment! You can cancel at any time by marking "cancel" on your statement or returning a shipment to us at our cost.

Free Newsletter!

You'll get a free newsletter—an insider's look at our most popular authors and their upcoming novels.

Special Extras—Free!

When you subscribe to the Harlequin Reader Service®, you'll also get additional free gifts from time to time as a token of our appreciation for being a home subscriber.

You'll look like a million dollars when you wear this elegant necklace! It's a generous 20 inches long and each link is double-soldered for strength and durability.

HARLEQUIN "NO RISK" GUARANTEE

★ You're not required to buy a single book—ever!
★ As a subscriber, you must be completely satisfied or you may cancel at any time by marking ''cancel'' on your statement or returning a shipment of books at our cost.
★ The free books and gifts you receive from this LUCKY HEARTS offer remain yours to keep—in any case.

If offer card is missing, write to:
Harlequin Reader Service, P.O. Box 609, Fort Erie, Ontario L2A 5X3

a rundown in her mind of what she would be evaluating when her breakfast arrived.

Among other things, a top room waiter—male or female—would use her surname, smile and be pleasant, prepare the food cart or tray for her to sit down and begin eating, and make sure everything on it was exactly what she had ordered. Blair planned to pay cash and note the serial number on the check. When her report reached Wesmar headquarters, the St. Martin's accounting department would be required to determine whether the cash was turned in.

Blair placed a wool skirt and silk blouse in the plastic bag provided by the valet service for cleaning and pressing. The skirt had a deliberate grease stain, the blouse an ink stain. She had placed a dollar in the skirt pocket to see if it would be returned.

Would the stains come out, would the dollar come back, would the valet come through looking like a champ? Though she wasn't really a nitpicking fussbudget, she loved being one on the job.

There was a knock on the door. "Room service," a muffled voice announced. Plastic bag in hand, Blair opened the door. Her gasp of surprise echoed down the hall. There was nowhere to run. Her next thought was that her disguise was incomplete. She hadn't put on her glasses.

Devastatingly handsome in dark suit and tie, Powers was standing behind a room service cart. "Good morning, Ms. Sansome," he said, "for the second time today."

Blair almost dropped the valet bag. "What are you—I thought you were—" She broke off to swallow hard.

"I'm filling in," he said, a half smile on his lips. "We're two waiters short today."

Impossible, Blair thought. General mangers never did room service. Yet, here he was. And expecting a satisfactory explanation for her breakfast order, from the look in his eyes.

He nudged the cart. "May we come in?"

"Why—sure 'nough. Please do."

With nowhere to run, what else *was* there to do but open the door wide and let him roll breakfast into her suite? She racked her brain for something plausible to tell him. A cancellation? No. Two in a row would arouse suspicion. He was no fool.

He parked the cart at the parlor window that looked out on the Golden Gate Bridge.

"What happened to breakfast out?" he inquired, pulling a chair up to the cart for her.

She glanced nervously out the window at the fog-shrouded bridge and grabbed at the sudden lifeline it presented. She thanked her lucky stars that she'd turned the radio on. "A three-car jam-up on that bridge out there," she improvised quickly.

"Come again?"

"My client's right out there right now." Thinking fast, she continued, "He called on his car phone right after you did and said he didn't know *when* he'd get here."

"Oh," Powers said, looking too happy for words. "I couldn't help but wonder. So that's it."

"I called you back to accept your offer, but your line just rang 'n' rang," she went on foolishly.

"Here, sit down." He offered the chair. She sat. He pulled a chair up for himself and faced her across the cart. "I called you from room service, not my suite," he explained.

"Oh," she said, relieved that she hadn't made a tactical error. "Good thing I didn't go traipsin' down to the coffee shop to find you, then."

He grinned. "Yeah. Good thing. You'd have found Pop there, though, yakking it up with my chief of security. By the time Pop leaves, he'll know every employee in the place better than I do. Wait and see."

Blair watched him remove the dome covers from the plates on the cart. She wanted to close her eyes, for he was so good to look at. His eyes were russet in the flat, foggy light from the window. His hair was thick and wheaty blond. She knew that hair the same color swirled on his upper chest, surrounded his sex, sprinkled his legs.

He caught her looking at him and grinned. "Eat," he said. "Go ahead. I'll just keep you company."

"What about your fillin' in for room service?"

He placed her fork in her hand. "I'm not really filling in. I just happened to be there when your order came in and thought, 'Why not?'" He poured coffee into her cup. "Lucky I did, eh? This way we can chat, get really acquainted."

As unlucky as it was, Blair couldn't help feeling fortunate to have Powers Knight seated across her breakfast table. It felt so good to be with a man like him. His energy and warmth were infectious, his smile a blessing. *Keep thinking like that, sugar magnolia*, she thought, *and you'll be falling in love before you can say rebel yell*.

"So," he said, "how is Seattle since I last saw it?"

"Growin'." Blair sipped her coffee. "Gettin' mighty expensive with Californians buyin' in to escape the real estate prices down here."

"That can't be bad for your business. CPAs must be in high demand with all that finance changing hands."

She nodded, completely in the dark about Seattle's need for certified public accountants. It was best to get off the subject of accounting right now.

"Tell me 'bout this hotel business you're in," she said, "and I'll munch away while you do."

He spread his hands in appeal. "Where do I start? I could talk all day about it."

"Start at the beginnin'," she suggested, and took a big bite of her English muffin so he'd have to talk.

"The beginning." He sat back and thought for a second. "Actually, I got into it through a woman I met. Well, not through her, exactly. Not a girlfriend. I barely knew her, is the best way to describe it, but she worked at the Four Seasons Hotel in Seattle. And that time I was there—remember I mentioned it in the limo . . . ?"

Blair nodded. It was all she could do to continue chewing. Her mouthful of muffin had turned to instant glue. She gulped some coffee.

"Anyway," he went on, "I dropped into the Four Seasons to sort of look around and just like that—" he snapped his fingers "—I got hooked on the idea of running a big, beautiful hotel. I had a semester left in grad school, not knowing exactly what I planned to do with an MBA, but after visiting that hotel I knew. Here I am, five years later, doing my thing." He smiled and looked at her, expecting a response.

"My word," she got out, "all because of a lady."

His eyes took on a faraway look for a moment. "Yep. She never knew it, but she was lucky for me." He touched the silver coffeepot. "Would you like more?"

"Yes, please."

He poured, looking at Blair. "With your glasses off you look a bit like her."

Blair jerked back slightly, having forgotten they were off. "Oh, my—" she exclaimed before catching herself and continuing, "*that's* why everythin' looks fuzzed, now, isn't it?" She moved to rise. "Excuse me just a moment while I get my specs."

He got to his feet first. "I'll get them. Where are they?"

It was best that he do it, she decided. Her legs felt a bit too boneless right then to walk on. "I left 'em on that bitty table right inside the bedroom door."

"'Bitty table.' I love it," she heard him murmur to himself as he headed past her.

In a flash, he was back. He didn't relinquish them as quickly as he'd retrieved them, however. "Fuzzed, am I?" Leaning closer over the table, he inquired, "How about now?"

"Now, you're . . ." *Within kissing distance!* She felt curiously unable to back away.

"How about now?" He leaned closer still.

Blair smelled coffee, butter, bacon, strawberry blin-tzes—and a light spice after-shave so seductive that more of *it* was all she ever wanted to smell again. She was vaguely aware of him slipping her glasses into his breast pocket.

"Are you . . . fixin' to kiss me . . . ?" she managed to breathe.

"I'm fixin' all right," he breathed back and then did just that. His lips, only his lips, met hers. They nibbled, coaxed, savored, convinced hers to do the same. They drew her toward him. She was entranced. He stood slowly, and she followed him up without breaking the contact. He had a taste like no other man she had ever kissed. She'd never forgotten it.

He rolled the table out from between them with his foot. Then he was holding her against him, lifting her to his kiss and pressing her breasts to his chest. He kissed her cheek, her earlobe.

"Sugar magnolia," he whispered into her ear, "for-give me if I'm ahead of myself again. If it's not what you want, tell me and I'll try, really try, to cool it."

Blair couldn't tell him anything. She could only slide her arms around his neck, glide her cheek along his and seek his mouth again with hers. In five long years she hadn't been kissed so. No man, it seemed, kissed as well, as thoroughly, as irresistibly.

He sucked her lower lip and ran his tongue over its fullness. He curled the fingers of his left hand to the side of her throat and traced a path under her lapel to her right breast. Weighing her in his cupped palm, he found her nipple with his thumb through her blouse.

"What do I do about you, sugar?" he murmured against her open, moving mouth. "What would you *have* me do?"

More, Blair thought. *Everything. And more. Now and for the rest of my life. For the rest of my life?*

She trembled on the brink of discovery. It was both statement and question. Blair became aware of her heart beating joyously under his caressing hand.

"Powers," she sighed. He swept her up into his arms then and placed her on the parlor sofa. They stared at each other, she perched on the edge, he on his knee before her.

And a good thing, too, Powers thought, for he was so hard he needed the concealment of his raised thigh. He took both her hands in his.

"Blair," he began. He cleared his throat and tried again. "Blair, overnight you've become special to me. But I don't want to rush you into anything."

Blair tried to orient herself. He was vibrating with sexual and emotional energy. She felt just the same.

"Am I rushing you, sugar?"

She sank woozily back on the sofa, searching for some sort of grip on herself. "It may be that we both are rushin' things. We barely know each other, after all." Thank heaven her accent was still intact. Little else was. She couldn't seem to fully remember why wanting him was a bad idea.

"There's an inner knowing, sugar. I feel it. I know you feel it. The world falls away for both of us when we're with each other."

She sat up and threaded her fingers through her hair in an effort to get her brain working again. She encountered the webbing of her wig. The feel of it startled every brain cell in her head back to full alert. What if Powers had furrowed *his* fingers through her false hair?

Dear God, what had she been doing kissing him and getting swept up beyond all thought of consequences? What was she doing right now, facing him without glasses?

"My specs," she said, flustered. She blinked and then squinted at him. "I can't see doodly-squat."

Powers pulled them out of his pocket and put them on her. "There." He settled his hands on her knees over her skirt. "How does doodly-squat look now?"

"Fine." In truth, he looked better than any one word could describe. Her jumpy gaze took in the breadth of his shoulders, the open-thighed position of his body in front of her. He was so powerful, so male, so easy to want.

"I'm trying to cool it," he said simply, squeezing her knees. "Just for you. How am I doing?"

"Not cool enough," she said breathlessly.

He moved his hands away. "How am I doing now?"

"Better."

"Cool is hell, sugar magnolia." He knelt there on one knee, looking at her with the fire of desire in his eyes. "Isn't it?"

The phone rang, saving her from replying. She got up and wobbled to the desk.

"Hello?"

"Blair, it's Lillian. Still practicing your accent, I hear. How are you, dear?"

"Fine as fine can be," Blair managed to respond. "And you? Better?"

"Bored as bored can be. I can't wait to get out of this hospital. The food is ghastly, a one at best on a scale of ten. How is the St. Martin measuring up so far?"

Blair shot a glance at Powers, who was sitting on the sofa, elbows on his knees, hands loosely clasped between them. He measured up better than Lillian would ever be able to imagine.

"Um, can I call you back?" she said. "Room service is here right now."

"By all means," Lillian said. "Get it while it's hot. Catch me later."

Blair hung up. "My client," she explained to Powers.

"Is traffic moving along again?" he inquired, standing.

She nodded. "It seems to be."

"Should I be moving along, too?" he asked. For a charged moment their gazes locked across the short space between them.

"A right good idea," she replied.

He held out his hand to her. "Walk me to the door?"

"A right bad idea," she said, clasping her hands behind her. "Thank you kindly for bringin' my breakfast, though."

"Walk me," he urged. He put his hands in his pockets. "I'm cooling off." Hands clasped behind her, she relented and accompanied him to the door. "Until tonight," he murmured, touching his lips lightly to hers. "I'll come by at seven to collect you."

After the door closed, Blair dropped into an armchair and gathered up her shattered self-control. She regrouped her scattered thoughts into logical sequences. Then she phoned Lillian back and told her nothing out of the ordinary had happened.

"Nothing," Lillian sighed gratefully in response to that news. "You can't begin to imagine the trouble I've imagined you getting into since you left here."

Receiver to her ear, Blair advised, "Imagine getting well, instead. I'm not in trouble." Powers *was* trouble beyond imagining.

8

AFTER CHECKING IN with Lillian, Blair went back to work. She taste-tested everything on the breakfast cart. Next, she pencil-marked a corner of each sheet and pillowcase on the bed to check whether the maid would change the sheets. Then she packed what she hadn't eaten into her purse, put on a light coat, and left the hotel for a short, head-clearing walk.

A block away from the St. Martin, a bag lady shuffled up to her on the sidewalk. "Spare change?" the woman inquired.

"Will breakfast help?" Blair removed the plastic packages from her purse. The woman took them with a furtive mutter of thanks, stuffed them into one of her four tattered, bulging shopping bags and shuffled away with her burden.

Blair moved on, hoping never to meet such a fate herself, yet glad to be of assistance in some way. Her own problems seemed less important, but they crept back into her thoughts as she walked along.

Powers. She clenched her hands in her coat pockets. She had been so helpless against his kiss, his embrace. " . . . The world falls away . . ." he had said. She had to admit that was exactly what happened each time they were together. Who could explain sexual attraction?

She walked up and down Post Street, pondering what to do about it. Twice along the way she called the St. Martin from a phone booth and left messages for herself to test the hotel's message service. Whatever happened, she had to continue her evaluation.

A big chunk of her task was to dine twice in each of the hotel's restaurants. After being discovered last night, she couldn't risk it again. She glanced into shop windows along her way, trying to think of a solution.

At a wig shop, she stopped and snapped her fingers. Eureka! Twenty minutes later Blair walked out of the shop with a package and directions to the nearest thrift shop. She emerged from the thrift shop dressed as a very senior citizen in a white wig, flowered crepe dress, lace shawl and gloves, opaque support hose, wire-rim spectacles and granny shoes. She carried a cane and a knitting tote that held her handbag and her previous disguise.

Perfect, perfect, she exulted on her way back to the hotel. She ordered a very early lunch in the grill room. She suffered a few tense moments as Powers and the maître d' passed through the restaurant and walked right by her table. Powers nodded at her politely, just as he did with every other guest. Perfect.

The leftovers from her grill lunch went into her knitting bag. Lunch in the penthouse restaurant followed without incident. When Blair returned to the lobby she put the concierge through his paces with a barrage of questions about city tours and several dogged requests for tickets to sold-out theater and symphony performances. The concierge passed muster.

Back in her room, Blair changed into her blah brown disguise and ordered a big lunch from room service. With a good part of three lunches in her bag, she treated herself to a leisurely walk around nearby Chinatown.

The sun had come out, brightening and warming the day. Blair felt as if she had stepped into China itself. She gave her food to a scruffy man begging at the ornamental gate at the intersection of Bush and Grant. Exotic little shops, restaurants and groceries lined the sidewalks. Blair saw everything from paper lanterns to Peking duck to root vegetables unheard of in American supermarkets—she was enticed and lured by the sights and scents of the wares of the Orient.

Like her fellow tourists, she gawked and marveled at everything she passed. She was coveting a $3,000 cloisonné vase in a shop window when someone grasped her upper arm from behind. She turned around, startled. The sidewalk seemed to tilt when she saw who it was.

"Well, hello there," Powers said. Matthew stood beside him, beaming.

"Uh, er, hello."

"Playing tourist?" Matthew inquired.

Blair shook off her initial shock and nodded. "I have a minute to look-see before my next meetin'. What are you-all doin' here?"

"After one won ton too many for lunch, we're walking it off." Matthew patted his stomach. "All the way from here to Fisherman's Wharf should do the trick."

"My, that's a mighty long walk to be walkin', isn't it?"

Powers chuckled. "That's what *I* told him."

"A long, meandering walk will do you good, boy," Matthew said, giving his son an elbow to the ribs. "Smell the roses, remember?"

"I'm partial to magnolias," Powers murmured, looking at Blair.

She immediately looked at her wristwatch. "Would you believe the way time's flyin'!" she exclaimed. "I've got to get hoppin'."

"Where? Can Pop and I walk you there?"

"Oh, no. No thank you. I'm headed thataway—to the financial district."

"That's not far. We could—"

"No, please go on meanderin'. I've got to hotfoot it fast to my meetin'." She eased her arm from Powers's hand and edged away. "Nice seein' y'all."

"See you tonight, Blair," Powers said with the most special, most tender, most killing of smiles.

Blair gave an ineffectual wave, turned away and hurried off before Powers could see how much that smile affected her.

"Blair appears to be as afflicted as you are," Matthew observed with another poke of his elbow to his son's ribs.

"I believe that she is," Powers mused, gazing after her. "I wish she didn't have so much business to do."

"I agree. If she had more time, *I* would do the fastest disappearing act you've ever seen."

"Don't disappear just yet, Pop. You've been good luck so far. You discovered her, you suggested cocktails last night, and you wanted lunch in Chinatown today."

Matthew swelled his chest out dramatically. "I *have* been instrumental, haven't I?"

Powers sighed and walked on with his father. "I wonder a little at all the business she insists she has to do."

"Wonder? Why?"

"Because I haven't seen her with her briefcase since yesterday at the airport. How does she do business involving legal paperwork without one?"

"Wasn't she carrying it just a moment ago?"

"Nope. She didn't have it last night in the coffee shop or cocktail lounge, either."

"Hmm."

"That's what *I* say, Pop. Very intriguing."

"You look all the more interested for it."

Powers nodded, smiling. "I've always been a sucker for a bit of intrigue."

THREE BLOCKS AWAY, Blair was hurrying back to the St. Martin. With Powers and Matthew headed for Fisherman's Wharf, she saw the opportunity to do some in-depth snooping without either of them stumbling upon her.

For the next two hours, she roamed the hotel. At the bell captain's desk in the lobby she noticed two bellmen chatting with each other while a female guest waited impatiently for help with her bags. She had a cup of tea in the tea room and "accidentally" left a blank notebook behind to see if it would turn up the next day in the security department.

She checked on several floors to see if the fire stairs were clear and accessible. Pretending that she wanted to book a reception for sixty people, she visited the catering department to test the staff's helpfulness and sales ability.

Finally, she returned to her room and checked the two messages she had phoned to herself earlier. One was correct. The other, supposedly from Ms. Bella Brown, was given as from Mr. V. Drown. Blair checked the daily maid service, discovering her pencil mark on one of the bedsheets. She then ordered an afternoon snack to test room service during off-peak hours. After it arrived, she flushed the clam chowder and ice cream sundae down the toilet.

"Chowder hot, sundae cold, but waiter didn't address me by name or set up seating," she recorded.

She then got busy transcribing her taped notes. As she did, she wondered how Angel Clare was doing. That dear little, sex-starved birdbrain. He wasn't cut out to be the Lone Ranger. The way things were going, she herself was living proof that the mating instinct was a mighty force, indeed. Maybe the most powerful in all of nature.

It was all Blair seemed to think about in her idle moments—and her working ones, as well. Here she was, thinking about Powers. He was the source, the cause of it all. She didn't know what she'd do if the situation got any stickier than it already was.

She knew what she *wanted* to do. Thank heaven the wig kept her from doing it. If there was one place a woman couldn't successfully wear a wig, it was in bed with a man. Moreover, it did help to be in love with the man first before getting that intimate. Well, maybe she was a little bit in love already.

Another thing Blair *wanted* to do was to buy a nice dress for tonight. She fingered the collar of her dumpy brown suit. Beautiful clothes had always been her weakness. What woman wouldn't want to look a little nicer than usual for the man she might have fallen a little in love with?

Blair turned off her recorder. A dress. It would lift her spirits just to buy one. She didn't *have* to wear it tonight. That would be courting disaster.

Vowing that she'd just buy a dress—and not wear it—she left the hotel and paid a quick visit to a nearby boutique. There she found the perfect dress. It was midnight-blue and cap-sleeved and silk. Splurging, she bought a pair of black high-heels, plain to be sure, but flattering to her legs, nonetheless. Finally, she purchased a small vial of Eau de Magnolia at the perfume counter.

POWERS LET OUT A LOW whistle when Blair opened her door and stepped out in her blue silk dress.

"Guess who's going to love looking at you across the table tonight?" he said, taking her arm. "And don't think I mean Conroy for even a minute."

"You look nice, too," she got out somewhat breathlessly. Powers was wearing a navy suit, pale yellow shirt and silk tie. She'd been unable to resist wearing the dress, and she felt very much like a fair lady with him despite her wig and glasses.

They rode the elevator up to the penthouse dining room with several other people. Blair was glad of the lack of privacy. Powers was looking at her as if he wanted to kiss her senseless. That hadn't been quite the reaction she had anticipated from him when she had dressed for dinner, or had it? She touched the virgin pin she had made certain she wore and saw his eyes follow the movement of her fingers.

Bending toward her, he whispered, "I get the message."

Then the elevator door opened into the dining room foyer. The maître d' led them to a secluded table where Conroy was already seated. As promised, he wore a suit and tie. He rose to greet them.

"Blair Sansome, meet Pete Conroy, my chief engineer. You've already met, of course," Powers said. When they were seated, Powers signaled the waiter. "A bottle of Dom Pérignon champagne and the truffle pâté to start, Pierre."

"*Oui*, Monsieur Knight."

"It's kind of you to let us make amends like this, Ms. Sansome," Conroy said.

"And right kind of you-all to do this," Blair replied, with a nod to both men. "My. Champagne and pâté. If this doesn't beat all, what does?"

"Would you rather a mint julep?" Powers's eyes twinkled.

"Oh, no. I love champagne." That much was true. She reminded herself not to have more than one glass. The objective tonight was to get back to her suite in one piece. She mustn't forget it no matter how Powers made her feel.

The champagne arrived and Conroy's pager went off. "Whoops," he said, standing, "not that elevator again, I hope. Excuse me while I call in and check it out."

Powers watched him leave. "Go ahead and pour for the two of us, Pierre," he said to the waiter. "I'll pour for Con when he comes back."

"*If* he comes back, monsieur," Pierre commented as he poured bubbly into their glasses. "The main boiler, it give him big trouble all day. Maybe more tonight, eh?"

"Maybe, Pierre. I hope not."

With a Gallic flourish, Pierre served the pâté. "Bon appétit," he said before disappearing again.

"Might be we should wait a bit for Mr. Conroy to come back," Blair suggested.

"Might be we should toast blue silk in the meantime," Powers countered, raising his glass. "You do look entirely lovely, sugar magnolia, circle pin and all."

Blair blushed and raised her glass to his toast and then to her lips. Dom Pérignon himself had been reputed to have exclaimed after his first taste of bubbly that drinking champagne was like drinking stars. Blair was in full agreement. And gazing into Powers Knight's eyes was like looking at stars.

Conroy came back to the table in a rush. "As much as I'd love to continue here, I can't, Ms. Sansome. I'm sorry." He turned to Powers. "Trouble in the boiler room. I'll catch you later."

Powers half rose. "You need me, Con?"

Conroy smiled wryly. "I'll page you if she blows. Enjoy your evening, both of you." He strode out of the dining room.

Powers sat down. "Time to buy a new boiler, I think."

"Seems to me it would be worth it," Blair commented with a shiver. "What fancy hotel wants its guests facin' cold showers in the mornin'?"

He gave her a long look across the table. "Should I have had a cold shower this morning, Blair?"

"Might be we *both* should have," she murmured, twisting her fingers around the stem of her glass. "I came here to work, not get romanced."

"You're the first woman I've truly romanced in a long time. I'm liking it too much to stop...unless you..." He leaned forward and covered her hand with his. "It's happening fast, I know. Too fast for you, maybe, but that's how things go with me. I'm an all-or-nothing guy. I'm trying to change, but I'm having one damned hard time of it with you."

Don't change, Blair wanted to say. She didn't, though. She just sat holding his hand. There was nothing half-hearted about Powers Knight. He knew exactly what he wanted and she was it. She couldn't think of any other man she knew who would openly declare himself as Powers just had. He'd spoken without a shred of evasion or caution. She found that remarkable, magnificent—and more seductive than anything any man had ever said to her.

Then he did something just as seductive. He smiled and lifted her fingers to his lips. "Tell me you want to be romanced, sugar magnolia. By me."

"I..."

"Do you, sugar?"

Blair felt her head nod entirely of its own volition. She dropped her gaze to hide her desire, but she wasn't fast enough.

Powers raised his champagne to her. "I'll drink to that."

Her eyes met his. His eyes never left hers as they sipped. What had brought forth that flood of feeling, Blair wondered. Why was it so impossible to do what she *should* do, and so easy to do what she shouldn't?

"Tell me who I'm romancing, Blair," he said setting his glass down and taking up a forkful of pâté. "Tell me about you."

She couldn't tell all, yet she wanted him to know something of her true self.

She told him about bayous and the French Quarters of New Orleans, the levees and Mardi Gras. She told him about cobblestoned streets, cast-ironwork balconies, fountains and hidden courtyards and Creole and Cajun cuisines. Powers laughed when she joked that the first thing a Creole asks St. Peter at the pearly gates is "Where's the jambalaya?"

They ordered the salmon en croûte with asparagus dijon. Mindful of every untruth she'd already told, she continued chatting with him through dinner. He told her stories about managing hotels and growing up with his brothers.

"And how did you decide to be a CPA?" he asked when their meal was finished and they lingered over coffee.

"My daddy is one," she said, which was entirely true.

"You like the work?"

She nodded. "I do love my work."

"Just for future reference, is yours a portable profession?"

"Why are you askin', Powers?"

"Because transfer is a fact of life for me, Blair."

Pierre walked up right then, eying their empty desert plates. "What may I serve you? More coffee? More raspberry soufflé?"

Powers gave Blair an inquiring glance. She shook her head.

"Just the check, Pierre."

Within two minutes Blair found herself walking out of the dining room on his arm. On her feet now, she felt the effects of every bubble in the three glasses of champagne she had drunk effervesce to her head.

"Dinner tasted right wonderful," she told Powers. "Thank you."

"You're welcome. How would you like to *see* something right wonderful next?" he asked as he squired her into the elevator. The other occupants made room for them.

"What might that be?"

"The swankiest suite in the city."

"I wouldn't mind seein' that." The bubbles encouraged her to speak without thinking very hard.

He smiled and inserted a gold key into a gold-plated, keyholed elevator button. The elevator stopped one floor down. They stepped out into a small, plush-carpeted foyer where two spotlit oil paintings flanked a double-door entry. Unlocking the doors with the same gold key, he led her into a suite the likes of which she had never seen before.

"Far and away," he said, "this is the most expensive suite in the city. Eight rooms, 6,000 square feet."

Blair didn't have to pretend to be impressed. "How much would it be to stay in a suite like this, Powers?"

"It rents for roughly a dollar a square foot, plus the city hotel tax."

"But who could possibly be *needin'* eight rooms?" Blair asked as they walked over an Aubusson carpet through a vast, elegantly appointed drawing room into a circular wood-paneled library.

"Who else but queens and kings, presidents, secretaries of state, foreign ministers, billionaire tycoons," Powers replied. "You name the world leader and he or she has probably slept here at one time or another."

"Isn't this the livin' word," she breathed, trailing a finger over the gold-plated fixtures in the bathroom.

"This is the smallest of four bathrooms," he informed her, leading her on. "Wait till you see the game room."

"*Game* room?"

"You bet. You want a game, video or otherwise, you get it. You want to seat fifty in the dining room, you can.

You want round-the-clock maid and butler service, it comes with the suite. You want a fully equipped kitchen—" he led her through a swinging door "—here it is, complete with butler's pantry."

"I'm havin' a hard time believin' this."

"Pop felt the same way. I brought him through this afternoon after we got back from the Wharf." He steered her down a hall and opened a massive carved door. "Here's the master bedroom."

Blair almost rubbed her eyes at the sight of the enormous four-poster bed. At least a dozen pillows bolstered the headboard.

"King size-and-a-half," Powers said. "The sheets, the feather bed, the comforter, are all custom-made for it."

Blair sank her hand into the cream-white comforter. "That's surely six inches of goosedown if it's an inch, now, isn't it? And under that is a feather-mattress?" She rolled her eyes.

"Rumor has it," Powers said, unknotting his silk tie, "that something very special once happened in this room."

Blair watched him pull the tie free of his collar and stuff it into his suit pocket. "Why are you doin' that?"

"Because I've been wearing a tie all day and I'm sick of it," he said, undoing the top button of his pale yellow shirt. "It's nice to breathe again, finally. Anyway, as I was saying, rumor has it that the beautiful princess of a famous principality was conceived on this very bed on a night very like tonight."

He pressed a light switch on the wall, then curved one arm around her and drew her close as the lamps in the room dimmed all the way down. Bluish light from the full moon shone through the windows onto the bed. Blair had an image of the king and queen making love in the great, downy bed. She looked up into Powers's moonlit eyes and saw herself as the queen and him as the king. It was so vivid, so easy to visualize, so wrong of her to be doing so.

"Powers . . ."

He drew her glasses off and hooked them over the lampshade behind her. "The minute I saw your dress tonight I knew I had to bring you here. Midnight blue begs for moonlight."

Powers pressed his lips to hers and kissed her senseless. Her knees buckled, and he lowered her to the bed and lay down beside her. Blair knew what was happening, yet kissing Powers Knight was too much pleasure to deny herself.

She savored the silky feel of his thrusting tongue against hers. His thigh slipped between hers. His hand caressed her breast through the silk of her dress, and she arched up to feel his touch more fully.

"I want you, sugar magnolia," he murmured, pressing kisses down her throat to the first button of her bodice. Blair felt buttons giving away, felt his fingers move over the white lace of her bra. He rubbed and she sighed. He pinched lightly and she whimpered. He replaced his fingers with his lips and kissed her there, wetting the lace with his tongue.

"Don't," Blair moaned when his mouth left her for a moment.

"Don't what?" his husky whisper inquired as he slid her bra strap off her shoulder and bared her breast.

"Don't . . . be stoppin' just yet."

"I won't. Not yet," he promised, tracing the shape of her nipple with the tip of his tongue. "Just a little bit of love is all we'll make tonight. Just a little."

Powers meant what he said. He'd go only so far and no further. Tonight was only a prelude to the ultimate that would come later.

Not too much later, though. He wouldn't be able to hold off for long at this rate, for she was too alive to his touch, too responsive. But he would hold off until she was entirely ready, he had promised himself that.

So he held back, kept his hands above Blair's waist, contented himself with baring her other breast to the moonlight and his mouth. Soon, he knew, he would have to stop. Soon, after his fingers memorized the delicate structure of her shoulders and collarbones and rib cage.

Then he felt her unbutton his shirt. Her trembling fingers pushed the shirt aside and furrowed through his chest hair.

"I must," she whispered, sliding her palms against his ribs and around to his back. "I must," she repeated as her movement massaged, then flattened her breasts against him.

"Yes," he found himself saying to the surprise of her hot nipples jutting against his chest. "Yes. Closer, sugar, closer."

Powers held Blair tightly against him, pressing her to him, urging her mouth up to his again. This time she joined him in a kiss not tender anymore but rampant with sexuality. He knew he had to stop now, for soon nothing would stop them.

It took a few seconds, but he found the strength to break the kiss and hold her away from him. "When we make love, sugar," he said breathlessly, "we're going to make it right. Not like this."

Blair clung to him, disoriented. "What . . . ?"

"Not here," he said, sliding her bra straps back over her shoulder. "Not now. I don't have protection for us."

She lay still, regaining her breath. Her realization of what had happened grew as he buttoned her dress. Powers sat up and began buttoning his shirt. As quickly as she could, she scooted off the bed.

"I—I've never—I don't know whatever got into me." She adjusted the rumpled skirt of her dress. "I'm just terrible sorry."

"Why?" he asked, rising to his feet beside her. "Because you got excited enough to forget yourself?"

"Yes. I didn't mean to be unbuttonin' your shirt." She turned her back to him and smoothed her hair.

"Blair," he said, resting his hands on her shoulders. "I want you. You want me. There's nothing wrong with that except our timing." He paused, soothing her shoulder blades with his thumbs. "You do want me, don't you?"

The best Blair could do was shrug her shoulders under his palms. "I didn't come to San Francisco to have this happen, Powers."

"It's not going to end here, Blair. If I wanted to visit you in Seattle, could I?"

"I . . . don't think so."

"Why? Is someone waiting for you there?"

Thinking only of Angel Clare, Blair managed to more or less truthfully nod. She felt Powers stiffen behind her.

"Someone serious?"

She shrugged again.

"Blair, you don't kiss like a woman with a serious someone waiting in Seattle for her. Why is that?"

"I . . . I mean, he's . . ."

"He's got competition now, hasn't he?"

"I don't know what to be sayin' to all this."

"Do you make love with him?"

Why did some lies leap to the tongue and others not at all? "No, but I've known him longer than you."

He moved flush against her back. "You can get to know me longer, sugar. I'm free if you are for breakfast, lunch and dinner tomorrow. Or join Pop and me for nine holes of golf after lunch, if that suits you better. Take your pick."

Her pick, she knew, should be none of the above. As if it were disconnected from her mind, her mouth said, "Golf sounds right nice."

"Good. Pop will be pleased." He nuzzled her ear. "If we tee off at three tomorrow afternoon, will that fit your schedule?"

"I b'lieve it will." Her mouth had a mind of its own. Her body was having its own separate say in the matter, pressing back into the heat of the tall, male body behind it.

Powers slid his hands to her hips and held her against his to inform her of everything *his* body had to say. "And now," he murmured, "we'd better go."

9

BLAIR WOKE THE NEXT morning to a wake-up call from the hotel operator who said that a large package had arrived for her. Did she want it delivered to her suite now or later?

"Now," she replied.

In the few minutes she had before the delivery bellman came knocking, Blair got into her wig, contacts, glasses and a robe. She was taking no chances.

As she dressed, she tried to invent a believable excuse for being unable to play golf this afternoon. *No more champagne,* she told herself. *No more moonlight.* They made her do and say things she had trouble believing.

Golf! Had she really said yes to it?

Yes. She remembered that word slipping out of her mouth every time "no" should have been the answer. Perhaps a golf course was a safe place to be with Powers. She couldn't deny that she loved being with him. But in the cold light of morning, it seemed just plain dumb to have accepted the invitation. Now she would have to shop for golf clothes.

The "package" arrived and turned out to be a good-size box with a department store label. Powers Knight's handwriting was on the attached envelope. The note read:

Since you may not have come prepared, allow me. Tee-off is at three at the Olympic Club. I'll be by at two-thirty for you.

> Yours, Powers

In the box were sport clothes perfect for the golf course, and three pairs of golf shoes in different sizes, one of them hers.

Blair checked the clock. It was seven-thirty. How had he done it? *When* had he done it? She could feel in her bones that he was falling in love as only a Type A could, full speed ahead. She could feel herself doing the same.

Damn. She knew just what she should do with the clothes. Yet how could she send them back after all the trouble he had gone to? How caring, how thoughtful, how *romantic* of him. Damn. Feeling flooded with emotion for Powers Knight was even more frustrating than wanting to have great sex with him.

Flooded, frustrated, wanting, she began trying on the clothes.

IN HIS SON'S SUITE, Matthew said, "I thought we were playing golf on Thursday."

"We were," Powers replied, "until I talked Blair into joining us today. We can still tour Alcatraz this morning."

"I see. In that case, there's no better day than today to tee off, if you ask me. Is a headache in order for me after the first hole?"

"No. Stick around for all nine. With you there, I'll *have* to keep my hands to myself. Otherwise..." Powers trailed off, thinking that Blair's breasts in the moonlight last night had been all that Love's had been in the dark of a night long past. Until now he had longed for Love. He'd thought Love was the beginning and the end for him. He'd never gotten past searching for her. He'd never thought another woman would blot Love from his memory. Blair had changed all that. Now he longed for Blair as he had longed for Love.

Matthew nodded sympathetically. "I had a hard time keeping my hands off your mother, too. It must run in the blood."

"Mine's running hot, Pop. She's the one."

IF POWERS WAS THE ONE, Blair thought, she would be leaving her heart in San Francisco for sure. She could be mistaken, though, as she had been with Jason and Jeff. This romance could well be a shipboard affair, fluff and St. Martin atmosphere and very little else. It could well have all the substance of a champagne bubble.

Blair dialed Powers's suite to thank him for the clothes. When he didn't answer, Blair dialed his office. "I'm sorry, Ms. Sansome," his secretary said, "he'll be away from the hotel all morning with his father. May I take a message?"

"Yes. Tell him everything fits, and I thank him most kindly."

Blair hung up. Away all morning. No Powers. No Matthew. Did breaks come any better than this? Even so, she would take *no* chances. Being a little old lady from now through lunch would be her best bet. All it would take would be a hotel emergency for Powers to show up unexpectedly. She'd had her fill of the unexpected. By two-thirty, she'd be all caught up on her work schedule.

After her shower she rearranged the chain in the flush mechanism of the toilet so that it wouldn't flush correctly. Response-timing the maintenance department after her call to report it, she ordered breakfast from room service again. She made a call to security about the notebook she'd "lost" in the tea room the day before. Next she removed all but one facial tissue from the supply in the bathroom to see if the maid would check and refill it. Breakfast in the coffee shop followed to test the morning shift. She conducted one test after another, until it was time to get ready for golf.

Powers knocked at two-twenty-nine. "I got your message," he said. "You're welcome." He looked her over, his smile warmly approving. "Everything *does* fit, doesn't it?"

"That was a lot of trouble you went through. I do 'preciate it."

"You'll appreciate the Olympic Club, too," he said. "Pop's downstairs. Ready?"

They rode down in the elevator, stealing little glances at each other. She looked at the way his white knit shirt showcased every muscle of his torso and shoulders; he looked at the way her knit polo shirt rounded over her breasts. When she looked away from the golden hair on his tanned forearms, she felt him look down at the narrow, pleated slacks he'd ordered for her.

Blair was glad to see Matthew at the carriage entrance. His fatherly smile and casual chat helped defuse the tension between herself and Powers during the drive to the oceanside club.

They rented golf bags and clubs, and headed for the first tee. Blair noticed that the wind was rising. For a woman wearing a wig, wind was no godsend. She hadn't brought extra hairpins. She could only hope the air would calm.

It didn't. Every time a stiff breeze ruffled her hair, her heart stuck in her throat.

By the fourth hole, Powers insisted that Blair wear his windbreaker. The pucker of her chilled nipples against her knit shirt was driving him crazy. As much as he relished looking at them, he wanted more to touch them. It was no way to play golf.

Enveloped in the jacket, wishing she could wear it over her head instead, Blair sliced her next shot into a cypress grove bordering the rough. Powers followed with his own unintentional slice into the same area. Matthew hit a straight line drive down the fairway. With a smile and a wave of his hand, he headed down the green to follow his ball.

Powers and Blair left their golf bags at the edge of the rough. He couldn't help smiling. There weren't many better places to be than chasing golf balls in the trees with Blair. Except in bed.

"Lousiest shot I've ever made," he muttered.

"Me, too," she replied, leading the way into the grove. "I've swung wild, of course, but never like this. You'd think I didn't know pea-turkey about golfin', now, wouldn't you?"

"Pea-turkey," he repeated with an amused chuckle. "You do say the cutest things, sugar magnolia. Look at me grinning when any other time I'd be calling myself a klutz for slicing the easiest drive on this course. I'm working less and enjoying it, all because of you."

Blair didn't dare to look back over her shoulder at him. If she did, Lord knew what might happen here in the trees. Golf balls were what she was searching out, not moments alone with Powers. She was accutely aware of him behind her. In her mind she pictured his broad chest, his sunlit, wind-tousled hair. She knew what could happen in just one moment.

"Where *are* those bitty balls?" she fretted.

Powers pulled her to a stop by the hand and pointed to the right. "There they are. Would you look at that?"

And there they were, kissing each other on a carpet of cypress needles, lit by a shaft of sunlight. They might have been nestled together by a tender, loving hand. Blair couldn't imagine the astronomical odds against their landing side by side.

His hand tightened around hers. "Our own hole in one," he murmured reverently. "A good omen."

Blair sputtered, "That—it's not possible." It couldn't be an omen.

"It means we're meant," he countered, turning her to face him.

She grasped his meaning, yet hoped he didn't mean it that way. "Meant?"

"For each other," he whispered, taking her into his arms and kissing her, sliding his hands down to her back. He pulled her against him, molding her breasts against his chest. "For this, Blair." His hands slid further down her back, cupping her bottom, molding her hips against his.

Kissing her again, he backed her up two steps against a tree. He felt her fingers curl around his neck as she deepened the kiss, felt her knees quiver apart to permit the upward rub of his thigh between hers. She felt so good, so right, meant only for him. He covered her breasts with his hands, stroked her tongue with his as his thigh moved intimately against her.

The more Powers had of Blair, the more he wanted. He wanted to lie with her on the sun-shafted carpet of cypress needles and take her right there with the wind whistling through the boughs overhead. He wanted her pleasure and his in wild, equal measure. He wanted to claim and possess her. He wanted her to be his woman. He wanted to be her man.

"Ohhh." He heard her sigh when he slipped one hand under the windbreaker. And again when he brushed his fingers over her full breasts.

Powers heard her response, felt her response. With other women, aside from Love, he'd been in far greater control than he was with Blair. Self-possession was tough to maintain.

Control. Powers breathed deep and forced his fingers to stop. Moved them away from her warm flesh to rest on the cold, rough tree bark above her shoulders. Breathed deep once more and slowed the friction of his thigh where she was welcoming it. Finally he and she were still and breathless.

"Before you leave San Francisco," he said, pushing her glasses up, "we're going to make love, Blair Sansome."

"I . . ." Blair sucked in a ragged breath. It was impossible to move, he was leaning against her so heavily. It was imperative that she answer him. Protest. "I . . . can't. Really, I just . . ."

"You want to. You showed me that last night and just now. We both want to."

"I—"

"When the time comes, sugar, we're meant for it. Not here." He pressed his fingers to her lips and eased away from her. "Not now. I know how it should be the first time. You won't regret a thing when it happens."

"But nothin' should happen." Blair felt glued to the tree trunk, locked into his gaze, paralyzed by the power of her passion for him.

Powers clasped her hands in his. "It's already begun. You've been making love to me, Blair, with every kiss, when you let me touch you last night." His eyes went very dark. "We were making love thirty seconds ago right here. Wanting more is no sin, sugar. It's only natural."

"Wantin' more after only two days is *un*natural," she found the strength to retort. "What must your daddy be thinkin', I wonder?"

"He's thinking I take after him. He fell in love with my mother at first sight." A smile hovered on his lips. "My oldest brother was born nine months to the day after they met."

It wasn't what Blair needed to hear. His kisses, his touches, his overwhelming sex appeal were strong arguments against her paltry side of the debate. She could resist other men's kisses, touches, sex appeal, yet she went boneless every time Powers so much as looked her way. She saw now that his family history was in direct opposition to her cause.

She tried to come up with something to support her side. "Your brothers didn't go makin' daddies of themselves that quick, I'd be willin' to bet."

"You'd win if you did," he admitted with a slow grin. "But then they've always been more conservative than I am."

"I'm *very* conservative," she hastened to say. "Very."

He stroked her hand lightly over his thigh, asserting, "You were liberal a minute ago. Very."

She flushed. "I don't go around doin' that, usually."

"You can do it again the next time we're alone. I won't mind a bit." He touched her flushed cheek. "Why are you so embarrassed, sugar?"

"Wouldn't *you* be if you'd been doin' what I was doin'?" she mumbled.

"No." Pressing her hand against his thigh, he murmured, "Feel what *I'm* doing." He slid her open palm up to where his arousal pressed against the zipper of his pants.

Powers didn't know if that was where a man should lead a virgin by the hand, but it was the only way he knew to communicate that she wasn't alone in responding fully to the moment. He saw her eyes widen, felt her hand stiffen for a moment then mold to his shape.

"I'm as beside myself as you are, sugar. You have nothing to blush about with me." He lifted her hand to his chest and pressed it against his heart.

Both gestures were just like him, Blair thought dizzily. He was as artless as he was astute. As confident as he was considerate, as straightforward as he was sensitive. And oh, dear heaven, he was as sexually potent as she remembered. Even his heartbeat under her hand felt virile, inherently male. Powers was more than she could manage.

She pulled her hand away, saw him frown slightly. "We're not gettin' much golf played here. Your daddy has to be waitin' for us out there."

He considered that for a moment, then stepped back. "Right. We do have five holes to go, don't we?"

She nodded. "We'd best be gettin' on with it."

"Give me a second." He turned his back to her, adjusted his pants and stood with his hands on his hips, regaining control.

Blair pushed away from the tree and came halfway out of her wig. No! It couldn't be caught on the bark! She felt behind her. It *was!* Snagged!

She swallowed a gasp and jerked back against the tree, her fingers fumbling feverishly with the snagged strands, her eyes focused on Powers's back. She heard him pull in a deep breath, saw him jam his hands into his pants pockets.

"Give me *two* seconds," he amended.

Wild-eyed, glasses askew, spine arched, Blair fought to free her wig without losing it entirely. If Powers turned around right now, she thought, it would all be over. He would see that her hair was short and black, not medium-length and brown. As she struggled, she saw his shoulders lift with an extra-deep breath.

"Give me three," he amended yet again.

At that second, Blair got the wig unsnagged. She pulled it back down over her hairline, rushed her fingers all around to tuck in stray wisps. She felt it anxiously. Was it on straight? She couldn't tell. It felt straight. Oh, for a mirror and a few more seconds!

"There," Powers said, turning to her. "Fit to appear in public again."

"Me, too," she replied, fluffing her fingers through the wig hair as if nothing more than a few kisses had mussed it.

"Your glasses are all crooked," Powers said, setting them straight.

Blair's thudding heart came to a sudden stop as Powers gazed searchingly into her eyes. He traced her eyebrows, her lips and then the hair that framed her face. She held her breath.

"Guess what I want to do about our golf balls?" he murmured, curling his index finger around a lock of hair just below her earlobe.

"What?" she almost squeaked.

"Leave them just like they are, that's what." He grinned and pecked a tiny kiss on the tip of her nose. "Is that okay with you?"

"Fine as fine can be," she replied and then led the way out of the trees.

It was like emerging into another world. The wind had risen a bit more, but not so much that her wig was in danger. Blair only hoped that the remaining five holes would be played without incident.

She played the next four holes well, tying with Powers on her score for the round so far. Matthew led them both with fewer strokes. The breeze even died down. Everything was looking rosy as she poised her club for her last line drive down the last fairway.

It was then that fate struck again. Though she swung hard and straight for the green, it wasn't hard or straight enough. Braked by a gust of wind that swept up the fairway, her ball landed in a sand trap.

"Tough," Powers sympathized, lining up his own shot. He swung hard and straight and landed his ball on the green, as did Matthew.

Tough, Blair agreed to herself. She was thinking that she would end the game well over her own par for nine holes. She had gotten herself sand-trapped before on Seattle courses. Getting out wasn't easy, but she could do it with the right technique and the right club.

She chose the right club and exercised the right form, but she wasn't expecting another gust of wind. Just as she chipped her ball up-slope onto the green, a gust sprayed the sand from her shot back into her face. Her glasses protected her face—except for a tiny grain of grit that got into one eye.

It might as well have been a granite boulder. It caused a rush of tears and pain when it slipped under her contact lens.

"Aarrgghh!" Dropping her club, Blair went down on her knees in the sand and dashed her glasses off. Her eye smarted and tears gushed. She had to take the lens out and rinse the grit off in a lens solution.

What lens solution? Hers was back at the hotel. She rarely carried a supply around with her. Few lens wearers did. Here in the sand trap she had nothing to help her out. Nothing.

Just Powers and Matthew rushing down from the green to her aid. They would see that her contact lens was opaque brown if she took it out, and that her eyes were really sea-green. They'd also wonder why she was wearing contact lenses and glasses at the same time.

That couldn't happen, she vowed. It could *not* happen. She covered her eye with her palm just as Powers knelt down beside her. Clucking his tongue, Matthew knelt on her other side.

"Here, look up. Let me see," Powers said, trying to tip her chin.

Blair tucked her head down. "It'll float out in just a minute now," she snuffled, her sinuses awash with draining tears.

Matthew pressed a white, square-folded handkerchief into her free hand. "Use this, my dear," he urged. "It's clean."

She cupped the folded square over her streaming eye. Her other eye streamed, too, but not so badly. Powers put his arm around her. His fingertips wiped her tears away tenderly.

"Blair, let me look," he coaxed. "I'll get it out."

She shook her head. "It's washin' out, bit by bit." It was doing no such thing, of course. Bit by bit it was forcing her into an immediate choice between agony and removing the lens. How could she remove it, though? Where would she put it? She sniffed back her tears, trying to think.

Soft contacts needed moisture. Where was the closest water? The fountain back at the seventh hole? Too far. The clubhouse? Closer, but still too far. She'd have to hold her lens between the tips of her thumb and forefinger, and keep her eye closed. It would only be a few minutes before she got to a tap.

Perfect. She had to get the lens out without either man noticing. The handkerchief. Bless Matthew. She let it unfold as she wiped it over her eyes. Behind that shield, she quickly pinched the lens out and held it between her fingers. Oh, blessed, blessed relief!

Powers squeezed her shoulders. "Blair, can you see your way to the clubhouse with my help?"

"Yes," she assured him. Handkerchief draped over her hand and eye, she let Powers and Matthew help her to stand.

Matthew retrieved her glasses from the sand and slid them into his son's shirt pocket. "You two go ahead. I'll gather up the equipment here and wheel the bags in."

Powers helped her make her one-eyed walk to the clubhouse. Along the way, he soothed, "We're getting there, sugar. We'll get the sand washed out."

Blair just nodded. As she walked she reminded herself to look somewhat unfocused since her glasses were in Powers's pocket. She even managed a slight stumble on the clubhouse steps to make sure Powers had no clue that she could see perfectly.

"Easy does it," he murmured, shoring her up. "Just a few more steps to first aid."

First aid? Blair blanched. Did he mean an in-house doctor or nurse or paramedic? She couldn't submit to an examination. All she needed was a water tap and a mirror.

"Powers, I just need a moment in the ladies' room." Next, she got herself out of the curve of his arm and made a beeline for the rest room she had visited just hours before.

Powers followed close behind her, protesting that she needed sterile eye wash.

"Really, I'll be just fine." Shaking her head in vigorous disagreement, she cut off his protest by snatching her glasses from his pocket and shutting him out with the door marked Women.

She sighed with relief once she got inside. Two women were touching up their makeup in the plush powder room. In the bathroom itself another woman was washing her hands. Reluctant to rinse her lens while being observed, Blair tucked Matthew's handkerchief into her pants pocket, kept her head down, and used the basin farthest from the woman to wash her free hand.

The woman dawdled, primping her hair, tucking her blouse into her golf skirt. "Such a beautiful day, isn't it?" she said to Blair. "Not a cloud in the sky, or fog, either."

Blair nodded and smiled. She couldn't let her see that her eyes were brown and green. Would the woman never leave?

"Bit of a breeze, though," the woman continued, smoothing her hair after a close examination of it in the mirror. "I hate wind when my roots need a touch-up. Every dark root shows. Never go blonde if you don't want to be a slave to your colorist." She adjusted her collar, waved and left.

Alone finally, Blair peeled her brown contact lens off the tip of her forefinger and released a profound and heartfelt sigh. She wriggled her cramped fingers. After almost losing her wig and a contact lens, she was safe again. Two close calls, and somehow she had survived both without being discovered.

She rinsed the lens with water, not the best wetting solution, and got it back into her eye. Perfect vision again. Brown eyes. Thank God. Even the wig was on straight with no wisps of her own hair sticking out. She wasn't sure how she had managed that by feel alone.

It certainly hadn't been due to luck. Luck was in such short supply that she still had two nights and a day and a half to get through in this disguise. She had almost lost it on the golf course right in front of Powers. Getting rid of the wig and lenses would be a help. It would also be impossible.

She scrutinized her teeth just to make sure the concealer hadn't come unglued without her noticing. It was still firmly in place. She cleaned her glasses and put them back on. Disguised again. What a relief. She couldn't help envying the champagne blonde who had just walked out with nothing to worry about but untouched roots. Oh, to be just a bleached blonde with only dark roots to be uptight about.

Blair stopped short and stared at herself in the mirror. *Blond.* She visualized her own short, dark, sleek hair blond. She would still be as far from brunette as possible, and only her hairstyle would be similar to Love's. Her eyes would still be brown. Her features would still be overpowered by the glasses. She would have no need of a wig.

One big, huge worry would be gone!

Blair walked out of that rest room wearing a huge smile. Powers had been watching the door vigilantly. He leapt to her side.

"Are you all right?"

"Fine as fine can be," she replied. "Where's your daddy?"

"Out front having the car brought around. You're sure you're fine?"

She lowered her glasses an inch and batted her eyelashes at him. "Nothin' to worry your head about. I'm seein' just as clear as clear can be."

Yes, indeedy, she gloated as she walked out to the car with him. After a couple of hours in a Union Square beauty salon, her wig and all the risks connected with it would be just a bad memory. Redyeing to black when she returned to Seattle would be a piece of cake.

10

POWERS WENT UP to the St. Martin security office after he returned from the golf course. "Is the new camera working yet, Dom?"

"The technician's installing it right now," the security chief replied. He tapped a finger against a dark video screen on the double row of surveillance monitors. "Any minute now we'll have moving pictures from the lobby." He tipped a cigar ash into his empty coffee cup. "How was the golf game?"

"Great, Dom. I had more fun playing than working. That's a change."

"Was the lady along?"

"Yep."

"How's that going?"

"Well enough that I'll be spending my free time in Seattle after Friday."

Dom let out a slow whistle. "You with free time on your hands? I never thought I'd see the day. You're moving pretty fast, lady-wise, though, Powers."

"With only four days to make a lasting impression, wouldn't you?"

"Yeah, I probably would if the thunderbolt hit me as hard as it has hit you." Dom chuckled and then sat up straighter as the dark video screen lit up with a snowy picture. "Here we go with the movies."

The screen blacked out for an instant before coming into sharp focus on the main lobby.

Powers studied the action on the screen. A group of Japanese tourists was clustered at the concierge's desk. The informal lobby bar was doing a brisk business. The usual foot traffic passed to and fro.

"Hey," said Dom, pointing at the screen. "There's your lady coming through. Same suit. Looks like she's in a real hurry."

Powers nodded. "She said she had a meeting. She must be on her way." He leaned forward, his eyes narrowing as he watched Blair rush past the group of tourists. "No briefcase again," he muttered.

"No what?"

"Briefcase. She's not carrying one. Odd, wouldn't you say, for a CPA headed to a meeting?"

"What brand of bean-counter is she?"

"Litigation support."

"Legal stuff?"

Powers nodded. "Very legal, according to Roger up in accounting."

"I get the point. Legal means paper. Numbers mean more paper. That much paper needs a briefcase." Dom took a long puff on his cigar and watched with Powers as Blair walked out of camera range.

"What do you think, Dom?"

He shrugged. "If she was drop-dead gorgeous, I'd say you aren't the only stud in the stable."

So that Dom wouldn't have to say it, Powers said, "Since she's not, what's your best bet?"

"Hard to say. After three ex-wives who were too gorgeous for their own good, I only know about alimony. What do *you* think?"

"I think I'm going to keep a close eye on the lady, Dom."

"Your old man says you've been doing that since she came here in the limo with you." Dom grinned.

"A closer eye, then," Powers amended thoughtfully. "A much closer eye."

He chewed his lip. It wasn't only the missing briefcase that was bothering him. On the golf course earlier, he'd noticed that Blair's hair didn't move quite as hair should move in a breeze. He'd begun to suspect that she might be wearing a wig.

That was no big deal, of course. Women wore wigs for lots of reasons. His mother had occasionally worn one to work when she'd missed her weekly beauty salon appointment. Still, it made him wonder.

If Blair *was* wearing a wig, why was she wearing it? And why was she always going to business meetings without a briefcase? It was a mystery.

He felt a sizzle of excitement. There had been a mystery woman one night in his life. Since his experience with Love, Powers had liked a touch of mystery in a woman. It intrigued him, made him curious and even more interested, and he was *very* interested in Blair.

He'd never been one to believe curiosity killed the cat.

"BLOND," BLAIR MARVELED at the change. She'd changed into her green suit after the golf game and hurried out of the hotel.

Ninety minutes later she was back from the salon with her hair bleached, toned, conditioned and trimmed. With her brown eyes, her dental concealer, her glasses — and her changed name—she was still well-disguised. The only added clue to her true appearance was the sleek, feathered hairstyle she had worn for years. Even that was altered, though, by the shorter-than-usual cut and ash-blond color.

She was convinced that Powers wouldn't think of Love LaFramboise when he looked at Blair Sansome.

There was little danger of discovery now if she made love with him. Not that she intended to get that intimate. No. Things had already gone too far.

If they went further, couldn't he recognize her by touch? Five years was a long time, perhaps long enough to dim his tactile memory. He had, after all, touched her last night without recognizing her.

As she had often done in the past two days, Blair wondered what Powers's love life had been since their night together. Why hadn't he found someone to marry? The biggest question of all, why was he so attracted to the blah Blair of the past two days? She was stumped for an answer.

Blair started changing into her little old lady disguise. She knew why she was falling in love with Powers Knight. He was exciting, amusing, romantic, sexy and handsome. He was by far the best lover she'd ever had.

He was loving, and thoughtful with Matthew. His employees liked and respected him.

He overworked, and he hadn't taken a vacation in five years. He was competitive and hard-driving, but he admitted to those traits and was trying to change them. In two days she'd seen him take time out for his father and for her. True, he'd been a terror behind the steering wheel on the drive to the golf course, but the drive back had been better. He'd actually stopped at yellow lights on the return trip instead of racing through them as they turned red.

Blair was proud of the efforts he was making. She pinned her white wig on tight and put her wire-rimmed spectacles on. She smoothed the limp collar of her shapeless, flowered-crepe dress. She made sure the back seams of her heavy-duty support hose were properly crooked, stepped into her black granny shoes, threw on her crocheted shawl, and picked up her cane.

She was almost out the door and on her way to dinner in the mezzanine grill when the phone rang.

"Hi," Powers said when she answered. "What are you doing for dinner?"

"Meetin' a client."

"What about after dinner?"

"After that, I'm . . ." Blair tried to think. What was a believable business thing to be doing after dinner? Not a movie. Not a play. What?

Taking full advantage of her hesitation, he said, "I'm free, too. Where are you having dinner?"

"Um, a restaurant in—" where were there a *lot* of restaurants? "—North Beach."

"How about meeting me afterward, say around ten, at Tosca Café? It's right in the middle of North Beach—two-hundred block of Columbus Street. I'll be there with a nun I want you to meet."

"Am I hearin' you right? A nun?"

"N as in Nancy, U as in Ursula, N as in Nancy," he confirmed. "Can I count on you?"

Blair bit her lip and considered. Meeting a nun sounded safe enough, if somewhat bizarre. And there was no doubt that seeing more of Powers was tempting as long as the circumstances could be controlled. What better controlling influence than a woman of the cloth?

"Ten o'clock, sugar?"

His voice was so seductive, such a thrill to her ear. Her heart missed a beat. She wanted to see him, risks be damned. Two hours of golf with him hadn't been enough. Besides, she couldn't think up a reasonable excuse for having business appointments after dinner.

"Yes," she quickly decided, too tempted to say no. "Ten."

"I'll be looking for you."

Before she could tell him to look for a blonde, he hung up. So he had a surprise in store, she thought, and shuffled out to dinner on her cane.

AT NINE FORTY-FIVE, with two hotel dinners behind her, Blair arrived in North Beach by taxicab. At her instruction, the cabbie had driven her past Tosca Café for a look-see and then let her off a few blocks away at an Italian restaurant he had enthusiastically recommended at her request.

She entered the trattoria and asked to see a menu. Should Powers happen to ask where she'd met her client, she wanted to be knowledgeable about the restaurant where they'd supposedly dined. She would take no chances by merely naming the place, as it might be one he was familiar with.

She scanned the dining area and decided that she and her client had been seated near the back. The plush banquette in the far corner looked just right. She decided that she had very much enjoyed marinated calamari, radicchio salad, linguine al pesto and cannoli for dessert. Her client, she determined, had savored his carpaccio, insalata mista, saltimbocca alla Romana and zuccotto.

Four blocks later, she walked into Tosca Café and got her first surprise. It was more a bar than a café. The narrow room had a long bar lining much of the right wall and a grouping of dated chairs and tables at the rear. A large espresso machine gleamed at each end of the back-mirrored bar. A jukebox on the left wall played Placido Domingo singing something romantically operatic in Italian.

Powers was seated mid-bar on a stool. He wore dove-gray wool slacks and a crew-neck sweater that was a shade darker. A black knit cardigan was laid over the stool next to him. The nun, Blair surmised, had apparently repaired to the ladies' room to adjust her habit.

Blair came up behind Powers and caught his eye in the mirror. "You-all call me blondie from here on in," she said over his shoulder.

He blinked once, twice, then whipped around, his eyes wide with pleased surprise. "Sugar?"

"Do you like it?" She touched the feathery tendrils at her neck.

He didn't answer, just continued to look at her.

"Well?" she prompted.

Wonderingly, he lifted his fingers to her cheek. Transfixed, he pronounced in a husky, flawless, accented imitation of Billy Crystal's famous comment, "You look marvelous."

Blair felt her cheeks warm in response. Being regarded with such wonder by such a wondrous man was complimentary enough. It never occurred to her that the more attractive she looked to him, the harder he just might fall.

Her only thought was that it felt marvelous to be the sole object of Powers Knight's attention. The one man she wanted most in the world was the one facing her right now. The one. The right one.

"Here, sit down," he said, sweeping the black sweater off the stool.

Weak-kneed, Blair glanced at the sweater and then in the direction of the rest rooms. "What about your nun?"

He followed her glance. His expression altered from appreciative wonder to something Blair couldn't identify. Concealed amusement, perhaps? What did that smile mean?

"She'll be here in a minute," he said, helping her off with her coat. He pulled her stool as close to his as it could get and helped her onto it. "I hope you like her as much as I do."

"Me, too. I've never had the pleasure of meetin' a nun. How do you know her?"

"I met her right here at Tosca," he replied, that unidentifiable smile playing on his lips. "Would you like a drink?" At her nod he signaled to the bartender with two upraised fingers.

The bartender, busy at the espresso machine, caught the high-sign and nodded. He looked to be in his late sixties, with a lined, kindly face. She turned her attention back to Powers. "Since when do nuns go into bars?" she inquired in a low voice.

His smile widened. "This is San Francisco, sugar magnolia." He took her nearest hand and laced his fingers with hers. "Here, it's not so strange to run into a nun in a nice bar."

Blair looked around to keep herself from squirming on her stool in response to the warmth of Powers's hand. It *was* a nice bar, in a simple, uncluttered way. She had the feeling that she had stepped back in time several decades. The old clock above the entrance, the vintage jukebox, the bartenders in white shirts and black vests, made her think of the 1930s.

"The jukebox played only opera until a disco opened next door a few years ago," Powers informed her. "Now the box competes with the disco beat on dance nights.

Other than that, the place is the same as it's been for ages."

"How do you know so much about Tosca if you've only been in San Francisco a month?"

Powers gestured down the bar. "Mario. He's worked here since the old, old days. He likes to reminisce when it's not too busy."

"How did you *find* it? From the outside it doesn't really look like a bar."

"My security chief, Dom Borello, comes here a lot. He introduced me."

"Does he know the nun, too?"

Powers nodded. "Very well."

Blair glanced again at the black sweater now draped across his lap. Added heat suffused her hand and arm as he lightly rubbed the back of her hand over the rough knit. She could feel the hardness of his thigh under the sweater without any effort.

"So," she said, elongating the vowel to a perilous length, "nuns are still wearin' black in the 1990s, are they?" She was having difficulty forming words without stammering.

"Not this one."

Blair tried to equate his enigmatic smile with the matter-of-fact statement he had just made. She tried to equate what she had expected to happen with what was happening to her hand against that black sweater. It didn't compute.

She wet her lips with her tongue. "Where did you say she went?"

"I didn't say, but here she comes," he replied with a nod in Mario's direction.

Mario was approaching with a steaming, brimming stemmed glass in each hand. "Here she comes?" she repeated blankly. Why did nothing add up?

"One white nun for the signorina," he said, setting one glass in front of Blair, "and one for the *paisan*." He set the other in front of Powers.

"*Grazie, paisan*," Powers said.

"*Di nulla*," Mario rasped and returned to the espresso machine.

Blair blinked at the hot, milk-pale, frothy concoction she had been served. "White nun?"

"A Tosca specialty," Powers confirmed with a squeeze of her hand in his. "Steamed milk, brandy and a dash of Kahlúa liqueur."

Blair closed her eyes. She'd been neatly led into keeping a date with the sexiest man in the world to meet a nun in a North Beach café. Now there was no telling what the evening might hold.

11

BY THE TIME BLAIR LEFT Tosca with Powers, she had made the acquaintance of two nuns and heard quite a lot of his life story. He had told her a bit more about why running a hotel was so absorbing and exciting to him. A hotel was like a little city, he'd said, one he loved managing. Every day was different, hectic, each with its challenges and emergencies. The keener the challenge, the bigger the emergency, the better he liked his job.

In turn, she had told him all about Angel Clare and Fred the birdsitter. Powers had complimented her several times on her new hair color and style. During that time at the bar, she had pushed her role as undercover guest to the back of her mind. It hadn't been difficult to relax into simply being a woman on a date with a fascinating man.

Walking with Powers, she felt pretty and desirable and very much desired. The narrow, busy streets of North Beach seemed the most romantic place she had ever been to. Here was a tortellini factory, there an Italian delicatessen; here a Chinese bakery, there a coffee-roasting company.

Here was Powers with his arm around her shoulders. They strolled around Washington Square, laughing at little jokes they told each other. When they came full circle, Powers hailed a cab for the ride back to the St. Martin.

In the back seat of the cab, he sifted his fingers through Blair's hair and kissed her breathless. Warmed by the nuns, she let it happen, welcomed the blatant heat of his mouth on hers, invited the covert descent of his fingers from her face to her breasts.

"I'm crazy about you," he whispered to her, touching her under her coat. "Crazy."

Reality was suspended. Blair was vaguely aware of reaching the hotel, riding up in the elevator, unlocking her door. Or was it Powers who unlocked it? Yes. He walked in behind her. In dazed, slow motion she reached for a light switch. His hand stopped hers.

He shut the door, then slid the safety chain and the dead bolt into place. He walked up behind her and pulled her flush against him. The full moon spilled its muted light through the parlor window sheers, giving enough illumination for her to see his hands part the lapels of her coat.

"Blair," he murmured, stringing kisses down the soft curve of her neck. He slipped her coat off and let it fall to the floor. He dropped his black sweater. He cupped her breasts in his palms. He nuzzled her ear. "Blair?"

Blair knew what he was asking. She knew what her answer should be. Pressing her breasts into his palms and her bottom against his hips was not that answer. Cupping her palms under his was the wrong response, as well. Whispering "yes" was out of the question.

Yet she whispered it, pressing her breasts against his palms and her bottom against his hips. "Yes." Cupping her palms under his, she prompted him to unbutton her suit and blouse and to unclasp her bra.

Her flesh was freed to his stroking touch. He turned her around to face him and took her glasses off. She felt the cashmere of his pullover against her bare skin. She lifted her mouth to his for a deep, demanding kiss.

He kissed her, but his kiss held no demand, only a tenderness so cherishing that it demanded only tenderness in return. Blair was emotionally undone even before his lips released her, and he began pressing the same sweet caress to her eyelids and temples. She combed her fingers through his hair.

"I need you, sugar . . . more of you." He kissed her lips again, then the tips of her breasts. "I need to know you want more of me."

She gasped, trembled, offered up her softness to him without reserve. He took it without reserve.

Blair lost track of everything but what she felt—what Powers made her feel. Somehow their clothing—all but her panties and his briefs—joined the coat and sweater on the floor. Their kisses and caresses, once tender, became erotic and fevered. So fevered that the bedroom seemed half a world away, too far to journey. Holding each other up became impossible. Powers lowered Blair to the carpet the instant her knees buckled.

She lay back and parted her legs so his hips found a cradle there. He braced himself on his elbow and rubbed his chest against her breasts. She rocked her pelvis against his, cupping his buttocks with eager hands. He raised his head and gazed at her body.

"Beautiful Blair." His eyes were luminous in the moonlight, his whisper a throaty, husky sound. "Sugar magnolia."

Blair curled her hands over his muscled shoulders, stroking his warm skin. "Powers . . ."

"Again." He pressed his ear to her lips. "Say it again."

She did, then twirled her tongue in the hollow of his ear. He moaned and lifted himself up to look at her, his arms braced on either side of her. "Do you know what you're doing, sugar?"

"I know . . ." She drifted her hands down his chest, down to where they had not yet touched him.

He lifted his hips, inviting her touch. She lifted hers, too, inviting his. She outlined him through cotton. He outlined her through silk. His fingers slipped beneath the silk and found her hot and damp. Her fingers found him beneath the cotton, hot and hard.

Beep-beep-beep! Beep-beep-beep! Beep-beep-beep!

Their hands went stock-still at the strident sound. Silence followed.

"What—?" Blair gasped.

Powers groaned deep in his throat. "No. Not now."

Beep-beep-beep! Beep-beep-beep! Beep-beep-beep!

"What—" Blair gasped again, pulling her hand out of his briefs.

"My pager," he growled, sliding his hand out of her panties.

"Pager," she repeated blankly.

"That's the emergency signal. I have to—" he grimaced and rose to his knees "—call security."

He twisted around and grabbed his sweater. He drew a small, electronic pager from the pocket and pushed a button to silence it. He looked down at Blair regretfully and traced a finger over her cheek.

"Damn it all, but I *have* to call in. It could be a fire, or worse. I'm sorry, sugar."

He bent, placed a quick kiss on her lips, then rose and went to the parlor phone. He flipped on the lamp, picked up the receiver and punched in a number.

"What's the problem, Dom?"

Blair sat up, blinking in the lamplight. She heard Powers say, "When? How?" Disoriented, she glanced around. Clothes were strewn over the carpet. Her glasses, his belt, her pumps, his loafers. Her legs still trembled. She pressed them together to quell the longing to wrap them around Powers in open surrender. She felt the liquid heat of her readiness to make love.

She glanced at Powers. He was looking longingly at her as he spoke on the phone. He listened for a moment and frowned.

Realizing what she must look like, a near-nude woman half-sprawled on the carpet, Blair grabbed her blouse and threw it over her shoulders, then hurried into the bedroom where she threw on a robe.

A glance at her mussed hair and flushed face in the mirror reminded her of how much she had lost herself to the passion of the moment. She would have made love with Powers except for that beeper. She had no control where he was concerned, none whatsoever.

She glanced away and saw her granny shoes and her cane in the open closet. She heard Powers hang up the phone.

What if he walks in right now and sees them! She pushed them behind her suitcase and slid the door shut with a bang.

What if he sees the wig! Rushing into the bathroom, she stuffed the white wig into a drawer.

"Blair?"

He sounded as close as the bedroom door. Her heart was pounding. She cast a desperate glance around for anything else that might give her away. *Wire-rim spectacles!*

"Sugar?"

He'd stepped into the bedroom now. She rammed the glasses into her robe pocket and stepped out of the bathroom. He was fastening his pants. They did little to hide his still-aroused state.

"What?" she responded as innocently as she could.

"A front-desk cashier was just robbed at gunpoint. She's fine, but I've got to get down there."

He strode back into the parlor. Blair followed, smoothing her hair. He pulled on his socks and loafers. She turned his pullover inside out and handed it to him.

"Thanks." He drew it on over his head.

She saw her glasses and popped them on. "All the better to see you with," she quipped.

"You're what *I* want to see," he said, slinging his black cardigan over one shoulder and coming toward her. "When do I see you again, sugar?"

"I'm not sure. I—"

Powers stopped directly in front of her. "When?" he repeated, pushing her glasses up her nose. "Tomorrow morning? Tomorrow noon?" His eyes darkened, probed deep. "Tomorrow night?"

Blair tried not to consider how heavenly tomorrow night could be. She tried to ignore the million tightly strung nerves in her body that ached to experience the ultimate fulfillment with him.

"Tell you what," he said. "Call me tomorrow if you can break free. Have me paged if I'm not in my office. Track me down. I want to see whatever I can of you."

Blair felt his intensity in the quiver of his arms that held her close. She saw it in his eyes, in his expression.

"What about your daddy?" she hedged. "Don't you have visitin' to do with him?"

"Yes, but Pop can extend his stay and you can't." His eyes lit up. "Or can you?"

"Oh no. There's not a gnat's chance in a hurricane of me stayin'. I've *got* to go come Friday mornin', just got to."

"And *I've* got to go right now, sugar. Call tomorrow. Call. Okay?"

Blair managed a half nod, half shake of her head and watched him leave.

She took a cold shower that night. Never had she taken one longer or colder. She got into bed, and set her alarm for 2:15 a.m. so she could order a snack. Testing room service in the wee hours was another part of her job.

EARLY THE NEXT MORNING PDK got a call from OTD.

"I'm looking at an order here for a bagel and lox, a side of fries, a fruit salad and a diet soda," she told him. "She paid cash. The time was 2:26 a.m. Today."

He blinked. "Five hours ago?"

"Mmm. She's got some appetite, this B. Sansome. Did you get my list of what she ordered from here yesterday?"

"Yes. You're *sure* she ordered during lunch hours?"

"Without a doubt. May I ask again why you want to know?"

"Just keep me posted, OTD."

"Will do, PDK."

He hung up and buzzed his secretary. "If Miss Sansome calls, put her through no matter what—and get me a printout of her room account from the front office."

Within fifteen minutes he had the document on his desk. It listed room and tax for three nights, three service charges for long distance calls made by phone card, one local call and a valet charge. Blair's major credit card had been routinely checked and cleared. The only seeming irregularity was that no meals had been charged to the room. Unlike most hotel guests, she apparently preferred to pay cash for meals.

Powers found that odd for a business traveler. Why was there only one local phone charge? Just to see who would answer, he called the number listed and reached

Cuts & Colors Hair Design. "Wrong number," he said and hung up.

It made sense that she had called for the hair appointment. It didn't make sense that she had made no local calls during her stay.

He pushed back in his leather chair and rubbed his chin. The more unanswered questions there were about Blair, the more intrigued he was. He closed his eyes and relived the night before, right up to the damned beeper going off. He cocked his feet up on the desk, tilted his seat and settled back for another replay.

Blair's legs had been a revelation, her breasts sublime, her every sigh and moan an aphrodisiac. For brief moments he had been reminded of Love, but only because the resemblance lived in Blair's new hairstyle and the awesome beauty of her calves and thighs. She had been every bit as arousing as Love.

He grinned and leaned back further. Taking time out as the doctor had ordered was no problem with Blair to think about.

For the first time in his working life he was hardly working. Damned if he didn't even have his feet up and his eyes closed at the start of the day. Damned if everything about her wasn't just what he needed in his life.

ALL YOU NEED, Blair was silently lecturing herself in her suite, is a good lay. It doesn't have to be Powers Knight!

Unfortunately she didn't believe it. She had never been one for recreational sex. She knew women who were, and right now she envied them. She wished she could be so casual. She wished that just anyone would do, but it had to be Powers for her and Powers alone.

"Call me," he had said.

She stared at the phone, put her hand on the receiver. *Call. Say you're free tonight. Say you can see him. Say there's no one in your heart but him. Say you're falling in love as fast as he is. Say you want, you will, you must.*

She jerked her hand away and turned back to the report she was filling out. There was still work to do. She had to inspect two cocktail lounges and use the hotel's swimming pool and health club. She had to rent a car for one day and park it in the hotel's garage. It would have to be driven in and out several times to test the garage attendants. So much to do. Another dinner to eat. Another valet charge to rack up.

Her first valet service had been good except for the money that hadn't been returned in the skirt pocket. That hadn't been the only petty theft. The turndown maid had proved to have sticky fingers. Two dimes were missing from the change on the table.

She tried to concentrate, but her fingers inched to the phone again. She jumped when it rang right under her hand. It was Powers.

"Remember when I said 'call' last night?" he inquired.

"Yes."

"Well, I spoke too soon. Pop's hot to see Sausalito and Tiburon today. We're leaving in a few minutes to wander around over there." He paused. "Any chance you could join us?"

"Not a gnat's chance in a vacuum cleaner."

He chuckled. "Just thought I'd ask." He paused again. "How's tonight looking?"

"Busy, busy, busy."

"All night long?"

This time the lull was hers. "Not *all* night," she replied as temporary insanity seized her tongue. "You could drop by around ten if you felt like it."

"I'll feel like it. Until ten . . ." He clicked off.

Blair put the phone down, her heart racing. *Ten.* The word had passed her lips. She'd heard it with her own ears. *Ten!*

"TEN TO ONE YOU'RE SEEING Blair tonight," Matthew said as Powers drove across the Golden Gate Bridge to Sausalito.

"What tells you that?"

"The five accidents we've almost had," Matthew replied, tightening his seat belt. "They were closer calls than usual, even for you. You're seeing her, all right, and you can't wait."

"I'll get you there and back in one piece, Pop."

"You did far better with Blair along for the ride yesterday."

Powers nodded. "I do better at everything when she's around."

"What are you two doing tonight?"

"Everything, I hope."

"You mean . . . ?"

Powers nodded and glanced at him. "Tonight is her last night here. I don't want to lose her, Pop." He paused. "Don't call me first thing in the morning."

"I wouldn't think of it, son," Matthew said, breaking into a big, sunny smile.

12

BLAIR KNEW SHE WAS cutting her swim too close to three o'clock for comfort. It had taken forever to get the car turned back in to the car rental agency. Now she was at the indoor pool an hour later than she had planned to be.

Wearing a sea-green one-piece that matched her eyes, she dived in and swam a few laps. The water was clear and sparkling, the temperature not too warm or too cold. The ladders at the deep end and the steps at the shallow end were slip-proofed. The pool was in prime condition.

There were three other swimmers, a young couple and their toddler. At the end of each lap, Blair emerged momentarily to check for any sign of Powers or Matthew. She was especially anxious because she wasn't wearing her brown contacts.

Without swim goggles, she couldn't risk losing her contacts in the pool. She was nearsighted without them so things looked fuzzy. Even so, she had no fear of not recognizing Powers. He was too tall, too blond, too charismatic to miss. She only feared him seeing the true color of her eyes.

Two more laps and she was out of the pool, drying off with a towel. A rather skimpy towel for a luxury hotel, she noted, holding it out in front of her to eye-measure its size. Right then, over the top of the towel, on the other side of the glass pool enclosure, she saw a blond head. Her heart stopped. She fumbled her real glasses onto her face. Powers!

Suited down in streamlined blue swim trunks, he was having a word in the entry area with the attendant. She saw him hold up his towel, just as she was holding hers. She saw the pool attendant spread her hands in appeal.

There was only one way back to the women's dressing room. Right past Powers. Blair draped her towel over her head and forehead, knowing she had to elude him. His back was to her. If he stayed like that, she could slip by. He had to stay like that. She gathered the edges of the towel shroudlike over her nose.

" . . . not the size they promised," she heard Powers saying as she approached him. "Not half as thick, either," she heard him add, as she edged soundlessly behind him on bare feet. "Not what we ordered," he said as he took a step backward almost directly in her path.

Heart in her throat, she veered, just missing him. Sucking in a tight breath, she sidestepped past his broad, beautiful back, his narrow waist, his cheeky buns, his long muscled legs. She touched the dressing room door. Almost there. Almost. One more step. She pushed the door open. Safe!

As the door swooshed closed behind her, she heard him emphasize, "Not what we ordered at all."

Blair got dressed and blow-dried her hair. Then came the problem of getting out without him spotting her from the pool. If he were in it. She wasn't sure he was. She eased through the door. A quick glance showed Powers standing in the shallow end with the young couple. He was holding their baby boy.

Blair couldn't move for a moment. Something about him cuddling that babe in his strong arms shot straight to her heart. She had never thought of him as a father, a family man. Now, seeing how natural he looked in the role, she felt a well of emotion. He smoothed a tendril of fine hair back from the tiny forehead.

His attention was solely on the child. Blair made a quick escape, her eyes misty, her heart full. She had always wanted children, couldn't imagine life without them, but the time had never been right. She didn't need that image of Powers and a baby indelibly imprinted in her mind.

Back in her suite, she'd have given a lot to have Angel Clare there listening to her troubles. "Bad news, Ange. I'm a blonde and he loves it. Even worse, I want his children. *His* and no one else's!"

ENJOYING A COCKTAIL in his son's suite before dinner, Matthew said, "Sit down. Pacing the floor won't bring ten o'clock around any sooner."

"The closer it gets, the longer it takes to get here," Powers muttered, slowing his pace. He checked his watch. Three hours and thirty-three minutes to go. He jingled the ice in his glass of Scotch.

"Drink your drink," Matthew advised. "You're making even *me* nervous."

"Can't help it, Pop. This is a big night. A lot depends on it. Everything."

"I wish your mother were here to see you like this. She despaired of you ever finding the right woman."

"I did, too," Powers admitted. "Until Blair I thought I'd missed my only chance."

"Only chance? Meaning?"

"Meaning I found the right woman once before Blair. Five years ago."

"When you were finishing grad school? Who?"

"Jason Aldren's fiancée."

Matthew regarded Powers for a long, silent moment, then puffed out a long, sympathetic sigh. "I see. The one in Seattle, I take it?"

Powers nodded. "There was no time, no way, for things to work out."

"You've never mentioned this before. Why now, son?"

"I don't know." Powers shrugged. "Maybe because I've been able to put it all in the past since Blair came along. Except that Blair looks something like her."

"You're certain you've put it all in the past, Powers?"

"Dead certain, Pop. Look at me. Do I look like I'm carrying an old torch?"

"Not in the least. You look like a man in need of a good meal before the night of his life. Where are we dining tonight?"

"At Dom Borello's place. He's cooking a mean lasagna tonight for the bachelors three—himself and us."

Matthew smiled. "If it's anything like the one he baked when I visited you in Chicago, let's go."

They had just left the suite and rounded the corner of the hall, when Powers saw an elderly woman leave Blair's room at the far end of the corridor. He saw her look his way, falter on her cane, then hobble quickly ahead to the elevator. He slowed, darting a questioning glance at Matthew.

Who was this senior citizen leaving Blair's suite at six forty-five?

"A client, perhaps?" Matthew murmured as they followed several yards behind her.

An amazingly spry one for her advanced age, Powers thought, as the woman hobbled faster. The elevator doors were opening. As she hastened into it, he called from halfway down the hall, "Ma'am, would you please hold that for us?"

He and Matthew sped up, but the doors shut before they could reach it.

"Thank you, ma'am," Powers muttered.

Matthew punched the call button. "Patience, boy. The older some of us get, the harder for us to hear." He touched his finger to the hearing aid in his left ear. "Bear with us."

"Sorry. I could have sworn she saw us." Powers looked back at Blair's door. "You don't think . . . ?"

Matthew shook his head. "Never drop in on a woman unannounced at the end of her workday. If she said ten she meant ten." After a moment, he added, "Anyone of any age can require the services of a good CPA, you know."

"You think she was one of Blair's clients?"

"That would stand to reason, wouldn't it?"

Powers was still trying to decide when the next elevator arrived to take them down.

AFTER RUSHING INTO the lobby ladies' room from the elevator, Blair was trying to calm down. This last close call had been too close. She shuddered at the thought. What if the doors had closed one second too late? What if Powers and Matthew had managed to get into the elevator with her? What if it had gotten stuck again with the three of them in it?

She opened her compact and powdered the perspiration on her forehead and upper lip. One more adrenaline overload and her nerves would be shot for life. Was that an ulcer she felt in the pit of her stomach—or just the triple-knot that had formed there after she'd insanely said "ten" to Powers?

Either way, it was going to make dinner one very difficult meal to eat *if* she dared venture out to eat it. Could she dare? Without knowing where Powers and Matthew had been headed, how could she dare? If they were dining out of the St. Martin, she could. If they weren't, they could be in any restaurant in the hotel. Was there some way to find out?

She snapped her fingers as the answer came to her.

Moments later she was on the house phone just around the corner from the ladies' room. "I'm an old, personal friend of Mr. Knight's," she said in a shaky voice to the operator. "There's no answer in his suite. Is there any way he can be paged if he's in the hotel?"

"Yes, ma'am," was the reply, "but he'll be away from the hotel until later tonight. My instructions are to page him only in an emergency."

"Oh, my. This is no emergency. Just an old, old friend. I'll try him later. Thank you."

Now, she thought, hanging up, there was only ten o'clock to worry about.

AT NINE-FORTY, BLAIR was worrying about what she would wear—and about what she had decided would happen tonight. She had already made an after-dinner purchase of condoms at the hotel drugstore. The sales-clerk had been admirably poker-faced during the trans-action, rolling his eyes as he watched her shuffle off in her granny shoes with a cane in one hand and birth control in the other.

Her granny garb was now locked safely out of sight in her suitcase. She was aware of how ludicrous it was to be dithering over what to wear. Total nudity would be most appropriate for a woman in her prospective situa-tion.

With last night to judge by, she knew Powers could re-move whatever she wore with breathless speed and ease. She also knew he could make love as slow and sweet as honey in January.

Weak with desire, Blair chose the silk. She dabbed magnolia perfume in all the right places. She placed sev-eral foil packages under the middle pillow, unplugged the bedroom lamps and opened the drapes. The night was clear, the moon still full. Powers wouldn't make any crucial connections between her and Love. Tonight, there would be no close calls. And no regrets, either, she vowed.

If getting heartstruck had happened in a few hectic days, getting back to normal couldn't be that much more difficult. After this second and last night in bed with him, she would go back to Seattle and forget, forgo, forswear everything to do with Powers.

He would get over being pie-eyed, too, once she left. Blair couldn't imagine him going for long without a lover. His ability to please her five years ago had been gained by experience, not abstinence.

The sound of the knock she was anticipating sent a thrill streaking up her spine.

She opened the door. There he stood, a fresh white magnolia in hand, an even whiter smile on his lips.

"Hi," Powers said. "Ready for a joyride?"

Blair felt her cheeks warm. Powers's smile and the magnolia were romance to her eyes.

His smile quirked up as she hesitated. "Did you think I meant something naughty, Blair?"

"Naughty enough from the sound of it," she mumbled, opening the door wider to let him in.

"I'm sorry. I meant a cable car ride. I thought you might like to go out. Maybe dancing, maybe a late show. Anything special you'd like to do?"

Blair took the blossom he held out and tried to look interested in his suggestions. It was hard not to look turned on by the sight of him. He was incredibly handsome, a dream of a guy, dressed in dark slacks and sweater with a butter-soft suede sport coat slung over his shoulder.

"It's chilly out," he said, his voice thickening as she stood staring at him wordlessly. "You'll need a coat for the ride."

"Yes . . . a coat." Blair's feet didn't move.

"Unless you'd rather—" he took a step closer "—stay here?" he finished hopefully.

She nodded before she could think. "Unless *you'd* rather . . ."

"Let's stay." He let his jacket slip from his fingers to the carpet and shut the door behind him. "I left my pager at home." He wanted to make sure she understood what was about to happen and had no misgivings. He didn't want to pull back as he'd been forced to do last night. "I've left my executive manager and Dom Borello in charge of the St. Martin tonight."

Blair smiled slowly at Powers and stepped into his embrace. He picked her up in his arms and carried her to the moonlit bedroom.

"Don't worry about a thing," he whispered against her hair. He'd brought protection in his pocket. Lots of it— just in case. He eased her onto the mattress.

Blair pulled him down onto the bed with her, eager for his swirling kiss, the hot glide of his tongue against her lips, the slip and slide of his hands all over her, the silky slide of his hard muscles against her palms.

"Blair," he was whispering, "sugar, I need you. You're special, different. I'm bowled over. Do you understand what you mean to me?"

She cupped her palm over his biceps, remembered him holding the child in the swimming pool. "I'm hearin' you," she whispered back, "and needin' you, too."

Her whispers and his became incoherent. He kissed her mouth from every angle and bared her breasts. Drawing her nipples between his lips, he sucked, eliciting soft gasps of pleasure.

As Powers undressed her with tender, passionate leisure, she pressed her lips to his collarbone and chest. He gasped. Her heart pounded when he slid her panties down her long legs, and slid his hands back up their smooth, bare slimness.

His touch molded her hips, rounded her bottom, brushed a tactile whisper over the silky triangle of hair at her center. Later he would stroke her there, when she wanted it more than anything in the world.

He lifted his hand to his belt buckle. Hers followed and helped him undo, unbutton, unzip, undress. There was so much he wanted for her, so much he wanted to make of this night. If she was a virgin . . .

He had to ask, but he didn't want her to feel insulted. He wanted to make every possible pleasure hers before the moment of truth.

If Blair knew none of the pleasures, he'd show her all of them. He led her hand down his body to his navel, then lower. In the moonlight, he watched as she traced his taut contours knowingly, without hesitation. What was that sound from her throat? Surprise? Shock? Fear? Fear would never do.

"Blair, have you . . ." What was the most delicate way to phrase it? "Have you done this before? Made, um—physical love?"

Blair marveled at his extraordinary restraint and the care he was taking. It was so unexpected.

His concern that she might be inexperienced made him a man to be adored as well as desired. How could she not love Powers for assuming nothing?

Unable to see her expression clearly, Powers tried to explain. "If you've never gone all the way, tell me. If you have, I'm not asking for a body count."

"I'm not a virgin," she soothed. "You won't be hurtin' me." She smiled up at him, heard his sigh of relief, felt his heart thud faster beneath her hand. "Will I be hurtin' *you*?"

He shook his head. "Only if we don't make love, Blair."

She moved her hand again. He stopped it a second time, held her palm flat against his abdomen.

"Powers, please. I want to touch you."

"Wait, sugar. Did he...did they...treat you right? Do right by you? I need to know. For you."

For you. Blair's heart soared. She couldn't resist a man who cared about her so much.

"Only one did," she replied. "A long time ago."

Powers kissed her temples, her eyelids.

"Lie back, sugar. Let me do right by you."

Blair urged him closer. He pressed her thighs apart and snuggled between her legs. He shaped her breasts to his kneading hands and sucking mouth.

"Do you love this?" he murmured every few moments. Her replies came in gasps and whimpers and words that said she did, she did. Lying under him, she couldn't see and touch him in all the ways he could see and touch her.

She could mesh her fingers in his moon-silvered hair, though, and she cradled the erotic movements of his head. Her fingertips traced the shape of his ears, made his nipples as hard as hers, kneaded the corded muscles of his shoulders and back and chest.

He slipped his hand between his body and hers and stroked her where he had stroked so lightly before. "Do you love this?" He caressed the hidden, pouted bud of her womanhood. She panted, "Yes, yes."

He slid his longest finger deep inside her, felt her tighten around it. "I'll be in you like this soon, sugar." He reached for his pants with his other hand. "As soon as I get into . . ."

" . . . This," she whispered, drawing the foil packet they both needed from beneath the pillow at her head.

"Sugar magnolia," he gasped in astonishment, then smiled. He touched her hair. "One minute you're a brownette, the next you're a blonde." He touched the packet in her fingers. "Now you're as prepared as I am. What next?"

His fingers continued to stroke her. She gasped, "Next I put this on you."

He knew he wouldn't withstand it if she did the honors the first time. Her touch would be too much. He was too taut, too strained, his need too volatile. He didn't move within her reach. Only his hand moved as he rocked the heel of his palm against her.

"Powers, please let me . . . if you don't I . . . oh, I . . ."

"Enjoy, sugar." The packet fell from her fingers. "Enjoy."

"Oh!" She gripped his shoulders, moved with his moving hand. "Oh, Powers!"

Wave after wave of sensation rippled through her. Her climactic cries sounded, slowed, quieted finally to soft gasps. She opened her eyes. All moonlit male, he was braced over her, poised to possess.

"Blair, look at me. Just look."

"I'm lookin' Powers." She lifted her knees, then reached down to guide him. He was sheathed, pulsing, throbbing. Her fingers curled around him. He was everything she remembered from long ago, as hot, as vital, as ready. She drew him close, to the threshold.

A swift thrust took him past it. Blair locked her legs around his hips, met his next thrust.

"Enjoy," she whispered, meeting another. And another.

His fingers clenched and unclenched in the soft flesh of her bottom. He plunged, drew back, drove in to the very deepest.

His groan of completion in the dark was one word: not *Blair*, not *sugar*, but *love*.

Or was it Love? he wondered in the brief calm afterward. Blair felt so like Love in the dark, in his arms. Her female scent was the same—which was impossible. His memory was playing tricks on him. Five years was a long

time. Far too long to remember accurately, he concluded, gathering Blair as closely into his arms as he
could hold her.

Love would only be with him in fond memory here-
after. Blair was now, she was his, she was all he wanted.

Proof of that, he wanted her again. Now.

Proof of that, she was urging him on.

POWERS WOKE SOMETIME in the night to sensation so delicious it might have been a dream. Blair was kneeling
under the bedcovers kissing the insides of his spread,
upraised thighs. His feet were flat on the mattress on either side of her, her palms were sliding up and down the
backs of his calves.

He closed his eyes and murmured, "Sugar."

"Mmm-hmm." Her throaty murmur was muffled by
the covers.

He felt her breath against him, the glide of her tongue
from his raised knee down along one thigh. He held his
breath. Her tongue moved up the other thigh to the other
knee. She did it again in reverse, skipping the halfway
mark each time. He smiled, drowsy, waking to the sensuous onslaught. She was a tease, was she? Would she
stop teasing halfway into the next glide and linger where
he was getting hard?

"Are you wantin' to go back to sleep, Powers?"

Such an impish, delightful tease. "Mmm, no."

"Wantin' *me* to go back to sleep?"

"No."

"Are you lovin' this, Powers?"

His hum of assent faded to a low moan as she stopped halfway and lingered. Her hair, her cheek brushed him there. Her lips moved over him, nipped kisses up and down. Her mouth opened, took him in, took him deep. Her fingers seduced lower down, shaping, weighing. He was hers, at her mercy.

She nodded her head and her mouth moved on him. Hot. Wet. His breath hissed through his teeth. Sweet agony. Sugar magnolia. He wanted her. Now. Framing her cheeks in his hands, he lifted her head from him.

"Come here, sugar." He threw off the covers and pulled Blair to his side.

"But—"

"No buts." Rolling her onto her back, he silenced her with a kiss. He lowered over her, settled between her legs, whispered, "I crave a taste, too."

Down her body he slid, kissing as he went. He lifted her knees, gliding his tongue from one to the other as she had done to him, teasing as she had teased. Once, twice, three times he skipped her center.

The fourth time he lingered, nuzzling her, warming her with his moist breath. Then moved away again. He came back to press against her. A slow whirl of his tongue made her whimper. A faster, wetter one made her moan.

Blair trembled with sensation, with desire. She flexed her hips up. The higher she strained, the faster his tongue swirled. She felt his lips, felt him suck gently, his tongue flicking at the same time. Ah, he knew everything, everything to do.

Blair knew what to do as well. She felt under the pillow for another foil packet.

13

THE MOON WAS GIVING WAY to dawn when Blair woke again. She lay looking at Powers in the blue-gray light. He was deeply asleep.

She imagined waking him up and telling him who she was and why she was here and how she had never really meant for any of this to happen but it had and it was all her fault for being weak and wanting him and now her heart was breaking.

Tears filled her eyes. No man would want to love and marry the woman in Jason's bed. She had played a role that night, tarty and brazen. Not quite a hooker, but a far cry from classy. Men's magazines and adult videos had been her cheat sheets for the image she had assumed. It still made her blush that she had said kinky, illicit things to a man she hadn't known. Even planning to say them to Jason had seemed risqué.

Men wanted women like that for one thing, and it wasn't for true loving. A wife who got risqué for her husband on occasion was one thing. What Blair had been that night was another. She knew that men made such distinctions. Women made them, too. Even worse, she hadn't known her fiancé from his buddy in bed!

She would curl up and die before telling the general manager of the prestigious St. Martin Hotel that she was

Love LaFramboise. It was disaster enough that she was a hotel evaluator in bed with him. In love with him, too.

She had only herself to blame. Her weakness for Powers had overcome her. Her loss of control had been total. The only thing to do was to take the earliest flight back to Seattle. Her business here was finished, the job done. It was time to leave—four hours earlier than she had planned.

She slipped out of bed, wincing at the litter of little foil squares. Powers didn't quiver an eyelid.

After a quick, quiet shower, she began packing her suitcase. The cane wouldn't fit. She slid it under the parlor sofa. When she was packed, dressed in her brown suit, ready to go, she sat at the parlor desk to write Powers a farewell note. After five minutes of staring at blank St. Martin stationery, she gave up and just made out a traveler's check to him in payment for the golf clothes he had bought her. A note was a coward's way out. She had enough guilt to deal with already.

She took the check into the bedroom. Sitting on the side of the bed, she screwed up her courage. After the night they had shared, she knew he might be more emotionally involved than she had suspected earlier. If so, she felt certain that he'd track her to Seattle unless she gave him good reason not to do that. The most compelling reason she could think of was another man. It would be her last, necessary lie.

"Powers?" She touched his shoulder. That broad, muscled shoulder. Little grip-of-passion crescents from her fingernails marked his skin there. She tried not to look at them, or at the whorled blond hair on his chest around the flat nipples that had peaked into tiny points under her fingertips last night. Her tongue upon them had made him moan. "Powers?"

Eyes closed, he rolled from his side onto his back. "Hmm?" His voice was thick with sleep. "Whadizzit?"

"Wake up."

"Sugar?"

"Yes. It's me. Wake up."

He reached for her, his eyelids fluttering. "C'mere sugar."

"I can't." She evaded his reaching hand. "I have to be leavin' here any minute now."

He lay still, very still, as if absorbing each word separately. "Leave?" he echoed, opening his eyes. "Who's leaving?"

"I am."

He propped himself up on one elbow, blinking. "Sugar, you can't leave. I love you."

Blair's heart cringed. Of all things, why had he said that now? He couldn't love her. She wasn't what he thought. "I've got to be goin', Powers." She took a deep breath. "But first, there's somethin' I have to tell you."

"Tell me your Seattle phone number, sugar."

"I can't." Oh, Lord. If he kept peering into her eyes through her glasses like that, she'd break into little pieces.

"Why not?"

"It's unlisted. The point is—"

"Sugar, have you been crying?" He was wide awake now, aware and frowning.

"Yes. From feelin' bad about leadin' you on and sleepin' with you."

He sat up. "Leading me on?"

She stood. "There's someone back in Seattle. The one I mentioned night before last." She visualized Angel Clare so the lie would be less black. "He, uh, lives with me, you see. We had a bitty tiff before I left, and I guess that's why I fell a little for you last night."

"A *little?*" He was up and out of bed, covers flying. Stark naked, he faced her. "You live with him? The one you told me you didn't make love with?"

She gulped. "Yes. This was all wrong of me to do. I'm goin' to forget it as fast as I can. You do that, too, Powers."

He caught her elbow as she turned to go. "Just a damn minute here. All I am to you is a one-night stand?"

"Not just that. I do lo-like you."

"You almost said it. You more than like me, sugar. Look at that bed. Count the wrappers. We tore them up together. That wasn't 'like' we made. It was love."

She didn't look. She couldn't. His eyes were heartbreak enough, fierce with hurt. He looked as if he would either beg her to stay, or strangle her. She pulled her arm out of his grasp, pressed the check into his hand and backed away.

"I'm goin', Powers. I'm sorry."

He matched every backward step she took with one step forward. Glancing at the check, he growled, "What's this? My stud fee?"

"It's for the golfin' clothes." Blair couldn't help noticing his magnificent, muscled body. Even at rest, his sex was a heavy, masterful sight. This was the last time she would ever see him. Blair took one long last look before she turned away and ran into the parlor.

She had said everything she could without breaking down. She had succeeded. Powers wouldn't be following her to Seattle. This was the end. Lillian would sign her name to Blair's report. Powers would never know who the undercover guest had been. The end.

She picked up her suitcase, her briefcase, her coat. "Goodbye, Powers."

From the bedroom doorway, he snorted, "That's all? Nothing else?"

"I don't see anythin' else to say." Opening the door, she paused and looked back one last time. "Except that you're . . ."

"What, Miss Sansome?"

"The best I ever had," she choked out. And then she slammed the door.

POWERS WORKED LONGER hours in the next week than he'd ever worked in seven consecutive days of his life. Anger was his fuel, bitterness his best buddy. His father had gone back to Vancouver sad-faced, shaking his head. His doctor, too, had shaken his head at the lack of improvement in his patient's Type-A symptoms.

Every St. Martin employee learned not to mess with the boss in a bad mood. Powers learned how to work more, sleep less, and inspire the fear of God in anyone who looked sideways at him.

None of it worked. He was exhausted and at rope's end. Seven days after Blair had left, a Friday, he barged into Dom Borello's office, a sheaf of papers and a bentwood cane in his hand.

"How much would you say she weighed?" Powers demanded.

"Who?"

"Who else, dammit?"

"Oh. Her." Dom gave him a guarded look. "One-fifteen at the most."

"Look at these room service tabs." Powers shook them in Dom's face. "Who eats like this between meals and stays at one-fifteen? Look at the phone calls on the account. Who keeps business appointments for four days and makes one local call to a beauty shop? Who supports litigation without a briefcase? Who comes in brunette on Monday and leaves blond on Friday? And *who* walks out after a night like that?"

Dom held up a hand to stop the barrage and asked his own pertinent question. "What's with the cane?"

"The maid found it in the suite the day Blair left. *I* saw an old lady leave there with it the night before. I spent the night in that suite. Why in the hell was this under the couch when the maid cleaned? And why in hell is the maid telling me she saw a white wig and old-lady shoes in Blair's closet when she made up the room before that?"

"Are you blowing off steam or looking for answers?" Dom warily inquired.

"Both. I smell a rat. I want her investigated. You're an ex-cop. Recommend a good, fast, discreet Seattle detective agency."

Dom flipped through a rolling file on his desk and pulled out a card. "Seattle's finest. You want me to ramrod this for you?"

"Would you?"

"Gladly. How much of a report do you want? Just the vitals—or a clear picture?"

"A clear picture. And I want it yesterday."

"It'll take longer than that. Promise me one thing, though. Don't punch me out if the report on Miss Mysterious isn't a keeper. With three ex-wives, I oughta know. Sometimes not knowing is better than knowing."

"I want to know, Dom."

"Don't say I didn't warn you." Dom picked up the phone and dialed the number on the card.

AT THE SAME MOMENT, Blair was sitting in a Seattle office having a heart-to-heart with her boss. It was Lillian's first day back at work since her appendectomy. Seeing the dark circles under Blair's eyes, Lillian had called her in to grill her. Before long, the whole fantastic story spilled out—from the night with Powers in Jason's bed, to meeting Matthew on the plane, to the flight out of San Francisco.

Lillian was distressed at Blair's emotional state. "I'm pleased with the job you've done, but you look as if you haven't slept or eaten all week, dear."

"I'll muddle through," Blair replied, dabbing her teary eyes with a tissue. "He's probably back to normal by now. I'll get there too, with time."

"Muddling is no way to live, Blair, when you're in love. You *are* in love, you know, however much you deny it."

"I'm in lust," Blair protested. "No better than the lady bird I bought for Angel Clare. Overnight they were tail-feather to tail-feather. Lust at first sight. That's Angelique, that's me."

Lillian smiled. "Angel and Angelique. That's sweet." She sobered. "But back to you. I can't help feeling you might make a clean breast of everything to Powers and come out of this better than you think. Some men are broadminded—pardon the pun."

"*Broad*minded is just what he was five years ago. *I* was the broad."

Lillian sighed. "As long as you didn't tie him up or haul out whips and chains, your behavior wasn't that inexcusable or unexplainable."

"I did tie him up," Blair confessed, blushing. "Not tightly. Just my lace bra around his ankles for fun."

"And he loved it, I'm sure. One kick and he'd have been free. My dear husband was like that, bless his soul. In thirty years of marriage we did our share to spice the stew, I don't mind telling you."

"You were married, Lillian. You knew each other. Powers and I were total strangers. I'd seen his picture in Jason's yearbook. He'd seen mine in Jason's apartment. That was all. Neither of us had a clue until the next day."

Lillian focused a very direct gaze on her. "On an unconscious level, you must have had a clue. Two strangers don't have to say as much as hello for vibrations and chemistry to match up. Give some thought to telling him and seeing what comes of it, Blair. Things happen, remember? Things happen right out of thin air when you least expect them."

THE REPORT POWERS received from Dom stunned him. Blair Sansome, formerly Love LaFramboise, had been born in New Orleans and moved with her family to Seattle at age nine. Her father was a partner in a Seattle CPA firm, her mother a housewife. They lived four blocks from Blair. She had an older, married sister who lived in Denver.

Blair lived in a Seattle condo she had owned for two years. She worked for an up-and-coming hotel/motel evaluation firm, owned two cockatiels, drove a red sports car, and had evaluated the St. Martin Hotel two weeks ago. She had never been arrested or jailed, paid her taxes on time, had many friends and no special man in her life.

Hair: black. Eyes: green. Height: five feet, five inches. Weight: one hundred and fifteen pounds. Eyesight: corrected with contact lenses.

Powers sat back in his desk chair, his chest expanding with a deep breath for the first time in two weeks. Blair and Love. One and the same. Here in his hands was the whole story. It answered every question. At last.

He sat in deep thought for a long time after reading the report. He knew what to do next. He'd been working too hard. It was time for a rest.

BLAIR DID GIVE SOME thought to what Lillian had said. It seemed Lillian might be right. After all, how could things really get any worse? She decided to call Powers the following Monday and tell him everything.

"I'm sorry," his secretary said. "He just left on a two-week vacation. A wilderness fishing trip. He'll be calling in from a ranger station for messages but can't be reached except for true emergencies. Do you wish to leave word for him if he calls in?"

"Please tell him . . . tell him Love called. Yes, that's my first name. He knows my last." Blair gave her unlisted number and hung up. Two weeks. If he called in, he would get the message sooner than that. She crossed her fingers. She hoped he'd call as soon as he heard her name.

FISHING WITH MATTHEW in the wilds of Vancouver Island, Powers asked him, "What do you think?"

"It's quite a story, I must say. Fate works in strange ways."

"Too strange. Now what?"

"You've heard nothing from her since she left?"

"Not a word."

"No message or letter since *you* left?"

Powers shrugged. "My secretary has instructions to call the ranger station only if Blair calls or the hotel burns down. The ranger's phone hasn't been ringing off the hook."

Matthew shook his head. "Call Blair when you get back from vacation," he advised. "You'll be rested, refreshed, better able to deal with the situation. Tell her you know. Tell her how you know."

"After I had her investigated? Pried into her private life? Hired a detective to follow her around for a week to scope out her life?"

"You had valid reason for it."

"I'd want to strangle anyone who had *me* investigated like that."

"Leaving things as they are means you'll have to live without her. Are you prepared for that?"

"Hell, no."

"Then you'll call when you get back, and hope she understands?"

"She'll most likely hang up on me."

"Nothing ventured, nothing gained, son."

SOMETHING VENTURED, nothing gained, Blair glumly reflected. It was a gloomy Friday afternoon. Rain, rain, rain. She'd been slogging through it all week. Powers's secretary had just confirmed that he had called in on Monday afternoon for messages. He'd probably used Love's message for fishbait.

So that was that. Her phone hadn't rung all week. She wanted to go home to Angel and Angelique and cry her heart out, but she had an appointment at the Four Seasons Hotel with the prospective buyer of a small chain of hotels.

Gideon Sindell had told her on the phone that he expected to close the Southwest deal any day now, and had invited her to pitch Carroll Management to him over high tea in his hotel suite.

Blair was glad that Lillian had assigned the client to her. Keeping super-busy was the only way for Blair to keep her mind off of Powers.

At the Four Seasons she checked her soaked raincoat and umbrella with the bell captain before going up to Sindell's suite with her briefcase in hand. Busy, busy, busy, she told herself. The busier, the better. This client had come along at just the right time.

She tried not to look surprised when Gideon Sindell opened his door to her. He was older than she had expected from his voice on the phone. She thought of Albert Einstein. His hair was pure white, and a walrus mustache obscured his mouth. He had Paul Newman's true blue eyes, Benjamin Franklin's square glasses and Bruce Springsteen's bolo tie.

Then she thought of Marlon Brando's voice in *The Godfather* when Sindell rasped, "Miss Sansome. How very nice to meet you." He shook her hand warmly and gestured with the cane for her to step inside.

Blair felt just a bit creepy when the door closed behind her. The suite was dark, with the drapes drawn. Only one lamp was lit in the parlor where an elaborate tea was laid out.

"Such a day out there," Sindell fussed. "We're not used to such in Arizona where I've lived since my rheumatism put a crick in my back and knees. It's best to be a duck here, I fear." Moving gingerly with the aid of his cane, he seated Blair in a tapestry chair at the tea table and settled into an identical chair across from her.

"Where did you live before that?" Blair asked conversationally.

"Oh, everywhere. My wife, rest her soul, was a Gemini, you see. They're a restless sort, those ruled by the planet Mercury. She led me a merry chase through life."

Blair smiled to hide a pang of regret. Matthew had once remarked that Powers was a Gemini. Powers had scoffed, saying no planet ran his life.

"Milk in your tea? Sugar? Lemon?"

"Just sugar, thank you, Mr. Sindell." He handed her a china cup and saucer.

"Please call me Gideon and I'll call you Blair." He served her finger sandwiches and petits fours, served himself and sat back with his tea. "Tell me about yourself. I do want to know who the undercover guest in my little hotels will be."

"I started as a management trainee at the Four Seasons," she began. "I left when I decided I was better at evaluating than managing. At Carroll Management, I—"

Gideon cut in, "Mrs. Carroll apprised me of your business background when I first called. Who are *you*, I want to know? Now, I myself am a rock hound for one thing. Lapidary is just one of my hobbies. I found, shaped and polished this stone myself," he said, proudly touching his turquoise bolo tie. "What about you, Blair? Any hobbies, interests?"

"Does breeding cockatiels qualify?"

"Cockatiels!" His luxuriant mustache curved up at the corners, then drooped. "The ones who make such a godawful racket an old man can't hear himself think?"

"No, no." Blair laughed. "The real noisemakers are cocka*toos*." She warmed to her subject. "They're bigger and far more aggressive. Cocka*tiels* are smaller, quite loving."

Seeing Gideon's blue eyes light with interest, she soon was telling him all about Angel and Angelique and Fred the birdsitter. He was so kindly, earnest and curious that Blair found herself speaking freely about herself. By the time she shared her desire to take sailing lessons, she felt as if he were a great-uncle or grandfather with whom she had always conversed on rainy afternoons.

He knew sailing and sailcraft and advised her to find a reputable instructor. "In fact," he said, "I have a yacht chartered for a noon cruise on Lake Washington tomorrow. Have lunch with me, why don't you? The yacht will give you a feel for whether you even like being confined on a boat. We'll talk business then."

"I'd love to," Blair said, since busy was the best way to be.

When Blair got home, the light was blinking on her answering machine. She prayed that the caller would be the man she loved. Holding her breath, she flipped the playback switch.

"Evenin', Lovie," her mother's voice drawled. "Any eggs from that darlin' Angel and Angelique, yet?"

14

THE YACHT GIDEON HAD chartered at the marina was big enough for a good-size party, let alone lunch for two. It came complete with captain, crew and waiter. Gideon was aboard, impressive in sailing whites and gold-braided yachting hat.

Before leaving home, Blair had made a last-ditch call to the St. Martin. She had asked the hotel operator if he'd called in after her last call. "Yes, ma'am," the operator had answered. "He calls every day, morning and evening."

Blair was feeling crushed when Gideon handed her onto the yacht and seated her at a table set for two. After a straight week of rain, it was a breathtakingly clear and sunny day. Blair felt anything but sunny inside as they cast off. She had to hide it from Gideon, though.

As they skimmed along, Blair told him what she knew of the history of the lake and its environs. She thought she was doing a good job of cloaking her emotions until Gideon gazed at her and said, "Feeling a bit under the weather, Blair?"

"Not at all." She pasted on her sunniest smile. "Let's talk about you and Carroll Management, shall we?"

"Let's talk champagne first, shall we?" said Gideon, summoning a white-jacketed waiter who served them two fluted, bubbling glasses.

"To us," Gideon toasted, touching her glass with his.

His roguish wink behind the square glasses and his lecherous chuckle gave Blair her first clue that Gideon had more in mind than a business relationship.

No, she thought, praying she was mistaken. Not this sweet, old, small-time hotelier. Not rheumatism and a roving eye, please. She took the smallest possible sip of champagne and set her glass down. She hastily took the proposed evaluation schedule from her briefcase. Though lunch hadn't been served, she could see it was time to do some no-frills business and get an equally no-frills message across.

"The way I see us starting out," she began, "is with a complete evaluation of—"

"Not yet," he interrupted. "Put that away and put a twinkle in an old man's eye, instead." A snap of his fingers brought the waiter again with plates of lobster thermidor.

Champagne and lobster thermidor suggested romance rather than business. On edge now, avoiding the champagne, Blair tasted the lobster. It would have been delicious except for the sight of Gideon running his tongue along his lips as he watched her eat.

Please, no. Not here in the middle of Lake Washington. Blair gazed longingly eastward at the Moss Bay marina where the yacht would dock before the return trip. It looked half a world away.

When Gideon began quizzing her about her love life as the meal progressed, she got edgier still. She answered his leading questions with shrugs and noncommittal answers. By the time chocolate-dipped strawberries were served for dessert, Blair was all nerves.

"It's the inner person, not the outer, that counts," Gideon declared, biting into a scarlet strawberry. "Today, with you, I feel like a young whippersnapper."

Blair felt the slide of his hand on her knee under the table. "Mr. Sindell!" She scooted her chair back.

He just chuckled. "There's more for dessert than strawberries, Blair." A snap of his fingers brought the waiter with a beautifully wrapped gift box.

"Open it," Gideon commanded softly, mustache twitching, his blue eyes glinting behind his Ben Franklins.

A quick glance over the deck rail showed Blair that Moss Bay was now close enough for her to jump overboard and swim to safety if necessary. "I'm afraid I can't accept a gift, Mr. Sindell," she declined as politely as she could. "Carroll Management never mixes business and pleasure."

"Open it," he insisted. "Then tell me I'm mixing business and pleasure."

Reluctantly, Blair opened the box. The tissue inside was as scarlet as sin. She felt faint as she unfolded it and discovered a black lace demi-bra, a matching garter belt with a red satin rose on each stocking clasp, sheer-black seamed stockings and string-bikini panties just as sheer with a rose embroidered on the front triangle.

Blair looked up at Gideon, appalled.

"Some women," Gideon said, gazing back, "worry what men will think of them for wearing such things. They worry that they'll be thought shameless, immodest, wanton. But I," he raspingly murmured, "am not such a man. I like a woman who doesn't always play it safe—a woman willing to take black-lace risks with the man she loves."

"With all due respect, Mr. Sindell," Blair said, rising from the table, "you are not the man I love. Nor is black lace lingerie the business I came here to discuss. Thank you for lunch."

Gideon rose, too. "Where are you going?"

"Back to Seattle in a taxi as soon as we dock."

"Why, Blair?"

Blair started to heatedly reply, then froze in mid-motion. The question had been asked full-voiced, without a rasp. The voice was not Gideon Sindell's. It was—

"Why?" he repeated.

It was Powers Knight!

"Trick or treat," he said, pulling off his hat, wig and spectacles.

Astonished, Blair sat down hard. She watched him peel away his bushy eyebrows, mustache and beard. "I don't . . . believe . . . this," she muttered.

"Believe it." Powers rubbed off the theatrical latex that had wrinkled the skin of his face, neck and hands. Looking himself again except for his blue contact lenses and stray bits of beard and latex, he settled back in his deck chair.

Blair shook her head. "What are you . . . *doing* here?"

"Me? I'm feeling as frisky as I did one night five years ago," he replied, reaching into the gift box. Drawing the garter belt out, he dangled it from one finger. "Are you?"

Blair gulped. "Powers, I—that night in Jason's—" She stopped as he undid a stocking clasp on the wisp of lace in his hand.

"The woman in Jason's bed," he said, "is the only woman I have wanted after that night, until she bumped into me again in San Francisco. I had a lot of un-answered questions after she left the St. Martin." He paused. "So I had her investigated. Later, when my sec-retary told me Love called, I knew what I had to do. So here I am."

Blair couldn't stop shaking her head in wonder. "You had me investigated?"

"Only because I cared so damned much." He leaned forward, his unnaturally blue eyes pleading. "I had to, Blair. I needed an explanation. More than you left me with at the hotel."

"I called to explain," Blair said, half rising. "The way I was at Jason's wasn't the real me. It was only for that night, only because . . . why are you nodding?"

"Because I knew him, too, before you did. The chase was his thing with women. After the catch, he always lost interest. You were only trying to get it back. I under-stand."

"You do?"

"Yeah." He grinned. "I love the way you tried."

"You don't think it was...that I was...out of bounds?" She couldn't quite name what she'd been that night.

He raised an eyebrow. "I was, too. We had the time of our lives. Remember?"

Blushing, she nodded. "I'll never forget."

"I loved it, Blair."

"Me, too."

"I love *you*."

Blair felt a bump as the boat came into dock. After it was secured, the captain called down, "Over or out?"

Powers looked at Blair. "They can take us back after a short break," he explained, "or leave us on board overnight if we want. What do *you* want?"

"Over," she replied. "I love you, too."

"Over," he called back to the captain, who promptly disembarked with the crew.

Alone now, except for the boats that surrounded them, Blair and Powers stood and came around the table to meet each other. Chest to breasts, hips to thighs, they embraced and greedily, hungrily, kissed.

"Sugar," Powers said, when they broke for breath, "could you work out of San Francisco?"

"I can work for Lillian out of anywhere."

"It will come to that, you know."

"I know."

"Let's make waves, then, Blair." He scooped the lingerie box under one arm and led her to the narrow stairway leading below deck.

On the last step down, Blair hesitated and looked up at him behind her. "There's more to me than sugar magnolia and Love, Powers. If they're all you want . . ."

"I want all of you," he confirmed. "Forever." Then he began to tease. "But if Sugar wants to drawl a word or two, and Love wants to call me loverman. . . ."

Fleet of foot, happy of heart, Blair cleared the last step down. "Let's be makin' waves right quick, loverman."

HARLEQUIN Temptation

Rebels & Rogues

All men are not created equal. Some are rough around the edges. Tough-minded but tenderhearted. Incredibly sexy. The tempting fulfillment of every woman's fantasy.

When it's time to fight for what they believe in, to win that special woman, our Rebels and Rogues are heroes at heart.

Cameron: He came on a mission from light-years away... then a flesh-and-blood female changed everything.

THE OUTSIDER by *Barbara Delinsky.*
Temptation #385, March 1992.

Jake: He was a rebel with a cause . . . but a beautiful woman threatened it all.

THE WOLF by *Madeline Harper.*
Temptation #389, April 1992.

At Temptation, 1992 is the Year of Rebels and Rogues. Look for twelve exciting stories, one each month, about bold and courageous men.

Don't miss upcoming books by your favorite authors, including Candace Schuler, JoAnn Ross and Janice Kaiser.

AVAILABLE WHEREVER HARLEQUIN BOOKS ARE SOLD.

my VALENTINE 1992

Celebrate the most romantic day of the year with
MY VALENTINE 1992—a sexy new collection of four
romantic stories written by our famous Temptation
authors:

GINA WILKINS
KRISTINE ROLOFSON
JOANN ROSS
VICKI LEWIS THOMPSON

My Valentine 1992—an exquisite escape into a romantic
and sensuous world.

Don't miss these sexy stories, available in February at your favorite retail outlet. Or order your
copy now by sending your name, address, zip or postal code, along with a check or money
order for $4.99 (please do not send cash) plus 75¢ postage and handling ($1.00 in Canada),
payable to Harlequin Books to:

In the U.S.

3010 Walden Avenue
P.O. Box 1396
Buffalo, NY 14269-1396

In Canada

P.O. Box 609
Fort Erie, Ontario
L2A 5X3

Please specify book title with your order.
Canadian residents add applicable federal and provincial taxes.

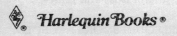 *Harlequin Books* ®

VAL-92-

HARLEQUIN
PROUDLY PRESENTS
A DAZZLING NEW CONCEPT IN ROMANCE FICTION

One small town—twelve terrific love stories

Welcome to Tyler, Wisconsin—a town full of people
you'll enjoy getting to know, memorable friends and
unforgettable lovers, and a long-buried secret that
lurks beneath its serene surface....

JOIN US FOR A YEAR IN THE LIFE OF
TYLER

Each book set in Tyler is a self-contained love story;
together, the twelve novels stitch the fabric of a
community.

LOSE YOUR HEART TO TYLER!

The excitement begins in March 1992, with
WHIRLWIND, by Nancy Martin. When lively, brash
Liza Baron arrives home unexpectedly, she moves
into the old family lodge, where the silent and
mysterious Cliff Forrester has been living in seclusion
for years....

WATCH FOR ALL TWELVE BOOKS
OF THE TYLER SERIES
Available wherever Harlequin books are sold